HOLY JESTER!

HOLY JESTER!

THE SAINT FRANCIS FABLES

WRITTEN AND
ILLUSTRATED BY
NOBEL PRIZE WINNER

DARIO FO

Translated by MARIO PIROVANO

HOLY JESTER! The Saint Francis Fables

Written and illustrated by Dario Fo
Translated by Mario Pirovano
All rights reserved.

ISBN: 978-1-62316-082-1

HOLY JESTER! is also available in OPUS e-book editions

A Division of Subtext Inc., **A Glenn Young Company**
P.O. Box 725 • Tuxedo Park, NY 10987
Publicity: E-mail: opusbookpubpr@aol.com
Rights enquiries: E-mail GY@opusbookpublishers.com
All other enquiries: www.opusbookpublishers.com

OPUS is distributed to the trade by
The Hal Leonard Publishing Group
www.halleonard.com

FIRST EDITION: 10 9 8 7 6 5 4 3 2

Printed in the United States of America.

CONTENTS

Whoever first applied the label "jester" to Francis must have been somebody with great imagination and subtle humor. Surely, the nickname was the poetic invention of a mischievous theologian from the 15th or 16th centuries. Or so I assumed!

But "jester" was not a moniker applied affectionately by historians or theologians, or sarcastically by his critics. The great historian Chiara Frugoni has revealed that Francis, in fact, adopted this appellation for himself!

"I am God's jester!" Francis declares not by way of apology but with pride and gusto.

At the beginning of the 13th century to dub yourself a buffoon or a satirical clown was provocative and dangerous, bordering on the crazily suicidal. Jesters were much beloved by the humble peasants, but hated and persecuted by the

INTRODUCTION

powerful, who condemned them to the pillory on every possible pretext. There were edicts against "professional clowns", the most famous of which, Contra Jogulatores Obloquentes, was issued by Frederick the Second of Swabia in 1220. "Obloquentes" means "slanderous, disgraceful, coarse, roguish ..." It's all there in that word! Frederick, by his edict, incited his people to attack any jesters performing at markets or public feasts. If the beating became a bit excessive, so that one of them died ... too bad! There were plenty more rogues where they came from! The Law was no obstacle to their blows, since jesters were not deemed civilized human beings and therefore not entitled to legal protection.

Francis didn't anoint himself God's jester to be provocative: he really was a bone fide jester with all the tricks of the trade up his sleeve. His harangues showed off all the techniques and routines of a master jester. Witnesses assure us that Francis possessed remarkable vocal powers, which allowed him to project his theatrical sermons to immense crowds, often exceeding 5,000 spectators. But more than his vocal prowess, Francis expressed himself through gesture. "He made his whole body speak," wrote an historian who attended one of Francis' performances for Pope Innocent III. The Pope was sufficiently moved by the animated friar that he sanctioned Francis to preach amongst the people in the vernacular.

In Rossellini's Francis, God's Jester, the opening sequence is in itself an all-time masterpiece of neo-realism. We see hundreds of friars, many of them very young, sitting, gabbing away in a great meadow. They are joking, playing and laughing … when out of the clear blue sky, it starts to rain. At first it is only a light shower, but drop by drop the shower becomes a downpour; great gusts of wind drive the rain into a frenzy: in other words, a typical summer storm. The friars, especially the youngest, run about the meadow delighted:

they wallow in the flood, rolling around among the bluffs; they lift up their habits to cover their heads; they fling their limbs about, just like a flock of birds … until they resemble crazed crows about to take off from the earth; out of this joyful frenzy, they simply disappear into the mist.

Francis would often begin his "services" with dance, transforming his sermon into a kind of musical entertainment, full of lively rhythms, drawing his audience in with stories of love and bawdy passion. Then out of all this earthly carnal love, he would change tack and introduce the purest, most joyful love we owe to our Creator. In this sense, Francis embraced the holy gesture with his whole being: de toto corpore fecerat linguam.

"I AM GOD'S JESTER!"

Francis appeared in hundreds of cities and townships throughout the Italian peninsula from the Veneto to Liguria, through the whole of central Italy, into the far south. His sermons and harangues dramatized the tragic conditions which brought suffering, desperation and misery. He ventured to Egypt and deliberated with the Sultan; he returned touched by the bonhomie of many "infidels" and disgusted by the total lack of humanity among the "Christian" crusaders.

In which language did Francis express himself? Hundreds of dialects, all mutually incomprehensible, were spoken in Italy at that time (Dante's "parlance of the people"). At the

IX

beginning of the 13th century there wasn't yet the least suggestion of an Italian language. The only means of intercommunication was Latin, spoken by the clergy and the upper classes. But Francis knew the composite, flexible language of the storytellers, which drew on idioms from the whole peninsula, full of onomatopoeic sounds, rich metaphors, and reinforced by a lexicon of gestures and by his extraordinary vocal gifts. It really was a 'passe-partout' of communication.

Producing emotion through laughter is one of the fundamental tenets of the Saint's living example. "This endless state of creation is a wonderful gift from the Lord!" Francis repeats throughout his ministry.

"Life is an incomparable prize. We, who have received this gift perpetually offered to us, must return it to Him with an uncontainable happiness. The infants who receive milk from their mother's breast, how do they show their gratitude if not by smiles and cries of joy? Therefore we, who are in every moment overwhelmed with grace and acts of love from our Creator, we must not forget what we knew as infants: to laugh and dance from joy!"

Francis' exhortation, to find grounds for ecstasy in everyday life, goes back to the most ancient popular religious traditions such as the rites of

the risus paschalis, or "Easter laughter." The resurrection of Christ was for centuries celebrated with comic skits performed by clerics disguised as fools. Francis draws on the Easter rite of the Exultet, a jubilant representation of the most playful passages of the Gospel.

Thomas of Eccleston in his English Chronicle describes the dinner of the friars around the fire: the food was scarce and the beer was like rinse water, but Francis and his followers nourished each other with funny stories. Instead of recipes for stews, they invented jests and paradoxes, filling their souls with resonant laughter.

The powerful are not capable of appreciating laughter, because he who undertakes the art of jollity and amusement, inevitably must snub the authorities, the generals, the notables and even the elect of God. It's no accident that in the sealed Rule of Francis, among the first suppressed chapters, the Saint exhorts his friars to always appear "jucundi", or jocular; to seek out the smile in every difficult situation, especially when offering succor to the infirm or desperate.

We must not imagine that the Saint of Assisi had discovered the value of beatific joy and mildness out of the cradle. The road to his conversion was paved with secular and sumptuous diversions.

> **"THIS ENDLESS STATE OF CREATION IS A WONDERFUL GIFT FROM THE LORD!"**

Pietro Bernardone's son had been outfitted to kill with the sword. He wore the arms and the insignia of knight, went through a terrible soul-searching crisis, and deserted. He threw himself into feasts and caroused with degenerate delights into the night with women of easy virtue. In his first awakening, he threw himself headlong into the rebellion against the nobles and the establishment. He suffered prison, and was obliged to rebuild walls and towers in the role of an apprentice and then of a skilled bricklayer.

Francis collapsed into a second crisis, and holed up in a cave to meditate and fast. When he emerged, he was like a prodigal son—throwing his money around and distributing the precious textiles from his father's shop to penniless paupers. He stripped naked through the streets publicly rejecting the trappings of world. He considered becoming a hermit tucked away in the mountains. But as much as he retreated, he could not abandon the community of men. Instead he went down into the hovels to give comfort to the lepers, the wretched, and the afflicted. He undertook the restoration, brick by back-breaking brick, of churches which had fallen into ruin.

Francis embarked on regular pilgrimages to persuade the popes to accept the Rule of Absolute Poverty. This fundamental principle required his followers' repudiate all money and spurn all possessions. Instead they embraced the obligation to earn a living doing the most menial labor. He discoursed on the Rule's applications and liberations with the learned men of the Church, the bishops and all his friars.

Francis was shocked and troubled by the unforeseeable consequences of his Order's success. More than ten thousand men petitioned to join his community across Europe. As his evangelical order grew, so did the pretension and manipulations of power hungry lieutenants. He was compelled to renounce the role of Chief of his own Order. He withdrew to meditate in the hermitage on Mount Verna with a handful of his followers. Ultimately and unavoidably he was once again drawn back to his beloved community where he yielded to the directives of the new bureaucratic superiors. Francis started to preach again, traveling to every city, from North to the deepest South of the Italian peninsula. People en masse flocked to hear him. His disciples who followed his pilgrimage often recorded notations of the whole performance.

Not a single line came down to us from these numberless writings of the Saint's disciples who documented his sermons and harangues. Forty years after the Saint's death, the new leader of the Franciscan Order, Bonaventure from Bagnoregio, decreed the destruction of all writings on the life of the Saint. Even Thomas of Celano's Leggenda, which had been commissioned by Pope Gregory IX, would be expunged. Every word spoken, written or dictated by the living Saint was to be obliterated. The actual words of the Saint written by his own hand, spoken from his own mouth, all these were expunged from the earth. In place of all these living words and primary sources, Bonaventura was appointed by the Chapter General in Narbonne to write a new, revised and sanitized Legenda Maior. The new official biography presented Francis as a sickly

INTRODUCTION

sweet figure more at home as a plaster statue in a middle class garden center than in the vibrant real life-and-death battles of his time. The true Francis had been crucified and then resurrected as a Sunday School Saint.

This massacre of the Saint's legacy would have included every speech dictated by the Saint in person and every transcription archived in the hermitages, in the schools and in the most far-flung parish churches. The General of the Order went so far as to award bounties to those who turned over codices and the transcripts in Latin or in vernacular. Instead of the hunters of beasts, mankind had become hunters of texts and ideas of peace and benevolence! The fateful censure by Bonaventure ignited a literal bonfire of writings and testimonies on the teaching and the life of Francis. Chiara Frugoni, the historian to whom we owe so much of our renewed knowledge of Francis, reports that this literary conflagration was one of the hugest in the Middle Ages.

Bonaventure cut and stitched together the three biographies by Thomas of Celano (written three years after the Saint's death), to produce a new and improved and unobjectionable Francis. No longer mad, unpredictable and innovative, this new and revised Francis was a meek and nearly angelic figure who flew high, often floating some meters above the ground. The New and Revised Francis was no longer to be found in dialogue with the desperate people of the earth but with the little birds chirping around bourgeois fountains. Here was an institutional Saint who constantly experienced heavenly visions and regularly received visits from the Cherub, the four-winged angel, a messenger of Christ, who impressed upon him the stigmata.

The newly renovated Saint stepped fully formed from the bureaucratic Vatican workshops nearly divine, more and more similar to Christ, perfectly pure and unreachable. He was a comforting, pacifying Saint; the provocative Francis who unsettled the soul had been stowed away.

It would no longer be necessary to follow in the footsteps of the recycled Saint; his newly minted sublime perfection would at most excite admiration: "Venerate, Do Not Imitate. Do not try these miracles at home." Absolute poverty, and the obligation of earning a living by working were considered "impracticable." The Order's rule book was revised to retire this central tenet into obscurity and eventual elimination.

When we admire a fresco or a painting on wood portraying episodes of the Saint's life by Giotto, Simone Martini or Pietro Lorenzetti, we must not forget that they derived their inspiration from the expurgated Legenda Maior perpetrated by Bonaventure. Any reference to the censored works of Francis was absolutely forbidden.

The great silence imposed on the works written during the life of the Saint and for forty years after his death, lasted a good five centuries. But we must not believe that the entire Order of Friars Minor meekly accepted this suppression of history. Those who were discovered in possession of non-canonical texts were risking severe punishment, including life imprisonment. Yet many friars preserved his words and continued their devotion to his original teachings by committing them to memory. The spirit of Saint Francis has been reawakened by the oral tradition through this miracle of renewed faith. The writings of Thomas of Celano and chronicles of other religious persons, which had been sequestered inside monasteries and libraries remote from Italy, have resurfaced. Other fragments keep coming to light.

One extraordinary performance lingers in the sacred air of history through the memories of several credible witnesses: Francis' sermon at Bologna in the summer of 1222. Bologna had for some years been at war with Imola and other cities of the Romagna; the conflict wreaked unspeakable massacres and wholesale slaughter. Parts of the city were burned and townships literally wiped out. Civil war raged between the noble families of the cities who attacked each other with unprecedented ferocity. At the urgent behest of his followers in Emilia-Romagna, Francis arrived in Piazza Maggiore on the 15th August. At sunset he climbed up on a makeshift stage cobbled together for the occasion. Thousands of people packed the piazza from every corner of the province.

Francis began to speak and at once turned the situation on its head: everyone expected a severe reprimand for the senseless killings. Instead the audience was dumbfounded as Francis delivered an oration in praise of war, miming terrific battles, playing out the encounters of cavalry and infantry, strewing about imaginary heads and juggling body parts.

The audience also expected the friar from Assisi would express himself in a fake local dialect with a few pseudo stock phrases in Umbrian. Instead he launched into a surreal rigmarole in the Neapolitan dialect!

The fables from Holy Jester rely on the overlooked episodes from the Saint's life together with ancient folk tales of the Umbrian countryside. I have allowed my imagination to visit and speculate about these dramatic scenes and episodes drawn from the fragments and threads of contemporary chronicles. From the patchwork of a jester's motley bag of tricks I have woven this tapestry of fables.

I wasn't present at these events! But you must trust me! When the original texts surface and the original Francis is reborn to us, you'll be able to say: "I have heard it all already!"

— **DARIO FO**

I

The

EXPULSION

of the

ARISTOCRATS

and the

DEMOLITION

of the

FORTY TOWERS

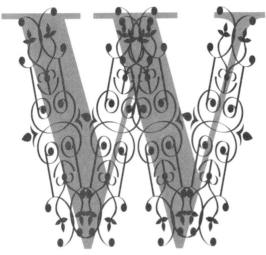hen Francis was just seventeen, he rebelled against his wealthy family and Assisi's powerful ruling class. He joined the rioting masses as they tore down the city's towers and chased off the aristocrats. The air rang with shouting . . .

"Pull, damn you! You are not pulling together!" Heave from your bellies! Now give the rope some slack. A bit more. Here we go! Raze it to the ground!"

"Here, she comes!"

"The humongous tower is falling!"

"Watch out, or it will fall on us!"

BATOOOOM! BABABLAM!

"Run for your lives!"

"Stones, rocks are raining down! The granite slabs collapsing!"

PUM! TA DEE ! PUM! BBBBOOOOM! PATOOM! POOOM!

"HELP! My foot is crushed!"

"See how the grand tower clatters into rubble before us."

" A great day's work!"

"We are not done yet. Let's go and wreck another!"

In just one morning the rebels managed to knock four towers down to the ground!

But the Mangia Family Tower was another story. Stubborn and proud stretching into the sky, it would not yield. The rioters surrounding it were like butterflies around an apple tree. The majestic tower that had stood for centuries was not impressed by these upstarts. Then the rioters scrambled to the pinnacle to secure their ropes. Others rushed up the steps, hoisting one rope here, three ropes there, ten ropes on the opposite side—hundreds and hundreds of ropes hurled all around the behemoth—and then:

"Heave ho! All together now! You gang on the other side, pull! Pull!"

"We've got nothing left to give. We're tugged out!"

"Heave! Will you not heave?"

"It's no good. Get a load of that mountain of mortar; Can't you see? It's not budging, it's standing erect like a giant...oak!"

A master mason interrupts: "It's simply too tall and the base is simply too wide. When we pull the ropes straight down, we're just anchoring the blasted thing more firmly in the earth. We're making it stronger, don't you see?"

"Time to give up! Let's go home, boys."

"Nobody said anything about giving up. First we pull sideways in one direction, then see-saw in the other. You guys, get

yourselves up the bell-tower. Then, throw ten ropes over the massive Mangia monolith."

"It'll be tougher job from up there. At least down below we can plant our feet."

None among the exhausted rioters made a move to climb the steep bell tower.

Francis rose to his feet and nine other young men followed him up the stairs, their shoulders loaded with hemp ropes. Once they reached the gargantuan arches at the peak, they threw the ropes over to their comrades across from them, who looped them around the Mangia tower and knotted them fast.

The other young men follow Francis' example planting their legs firmly apart, heels wedged between the columns of the arcade. One of the comrades placed himself above Francis, another below—a tangle of legs, columns, feet and taut ropes.

"All together!" called out the mason. "Pull those ropes like your lives depend on it— because they do! Zig and then Zag! Tug at full stretch!"

"Heavvvvve—Ho! Heave—Ho!" Francis sent up the chant which his gang picked up.

"Whoooops!"

All of sudden, one of Francis' legs slipped off the arch and got caught in the net of ropes. His foot planted against the column slips too—KABOOOM—He finds himself hurled out of the arcade, hanging onto his

rope and heading, like a bolt of lightning, straight for the massive Mangia tower.

"I'm going to be flattened!"

"We should have gone home while we were ahead!"

With a desperate twist of his hips, Francis just managed to miss the big tower and he gave a kick to the wall for good luck as he passes.

"Saints protect me!"

Clinging to the rope, he swings round the big tower, around and around in mid-air with a view of Assisi few mortals had ever experienced before.

Someone cries: "Hey, Francis enjoying the ride, eh?!"

But with each turn, the rope knots around the big tower, tightens, gets shorter and shorter.

"God! I'm going to get smashed!"

Another lucky kick, and he tumbles back the other direction going backwards. The rope unwinds.

"Heeelp! Make way! Damn, I'm swinging back ... toward the steeple. I can't stop myself. Oh no, Lord, spare me ... not the steeple bells!"

"VAVABAROOM!" He whizzes right into the steeple's arch, straight inside the cavernous bell! BOOM! BOOM! He grabs hold of the clapper but there is no lucky escape this time.

> "Hey Francis,
> enjoying
> the ride?"

BONG! BONG! BELONG! BELONG!

"My head! God, what a bang on the head! It's like a cave in here! Help!"

DING DONG! DONG!—Now the other bells begin to chime in concert—DING! DING! DONG! DONG!"

"My heaaad! Please don't DONG me any more!"

"Quick, quick—grab his legs, pull him out!"

Each time he swings back within their grasp, he slips away again. When they finally hoist him out of the bell's cavity, Francis' body is completely misshapen and twisted. His head is still shaking as if he were still clapping against the bronze bell. Two comrades try to straighten out his crooked legs.

"How are you doing, Francis?"

"Stop shouting, will you?"

"Let's get you down away from the bell tower. We'll take your arms going down."

"I'm just fine. I can make it."

"Careful. There are two hundred and fifty steps, Francis."

He begins to descend but instantly falters.

"Francis, you are just turning in circles on the same step. We will take you by the arms and you will walk."

DONG DONG! DONG! His head is an echo chamber.

He reaches the bottom, a comrade on each arm.

"Let me go! Let me go!"

But Francis cannot stand on his own. When his friends let him go, he collapses, twisted up like a ball of rags. He has one leg around his neck, the other one under his armpit, one arm twisted behind his back. His body sways back and forth to the rhythm of the bells up above.

"Pull him straight!"

"No, it's my leg!"

Finally, they rearrange his parts. All in one piece, he stands before them. But that's as far as he goes. They try to get him to move but it's as though he's a plaster statue from the chapel. Four of them shoulder him and take him home.

As soon as his mother sees him, being carried home like a stiff, she cries out: "My son! ... My son is deaaad! Ayhiiiiiiiiii!"

"Mother ... please ... do not scream ... I have twelve bells in my head!"

"Okay, boys," his mother whispers. "Take Francis down cellar where it is quiet and dark. I will tend to him there."

His comrades carry him down the narrow steps and place him next to the wine."

"Everything a man could ever want within arms reach," says one friend.

"Silence! Not a word!" Francis' mother scolds him.

Some poor soul passing by yells loudly: "Franciiis! How is it going? What a concert you gave us!"

"Ahhhhh! Quiet! Have mercy!"

So, there he remains for seven days: utterly still, stuck like an insect in amber, in complete and total silence. When he finally ascends into the light, he looks a bit tipsy, bewildered; he walks crookedly like an old man. On meeting him, his comrades tease him: "Hey, Francis, what time is it? Isn't it time you rang the morning bells!"

And he, like a good sport, plays along, going: "DING! DONG!"

Many years later, after he had become a Saint, everybody on earth, across the seas and beyond the mountains, knew about his blessed example. But some of these so-called "dearest friends' from the old days were going around saying:

"Oh, I remember the day Francis was flooded by divine Grace; he got banged upside the head inside the great bell. Yup, that was the day of the Great Bang. After that, he was never the same again. He walked around dazed, face up, always looking up at the sky. People say he was communing with the birds and the angels and such. But want to know the truth? He was trying to avoid another Great Bang!"

Francis smiled and said to the moon: "Hallo, sister!', then to the stars: "Little sisters ...;" to the sun: "Hallo, brother;" to the earth: "Mother earth." All one wondrous family!

He also conversed with the animals, with the birds, with the horses, the wolves and even the ants, saying: "Nice little ants, sweet little animals ... little beasts all in a line, so orderly ... trillillila trillillila!" Then he blessed them, and walked off but because he was looking up at the sky, he forgot the blessed little ants and stomped all over them!

The EXPULSION of the ARISTOCRATS

II

The

BATTLE
AGAINST

the

CITIZENS

of

PERUGIA

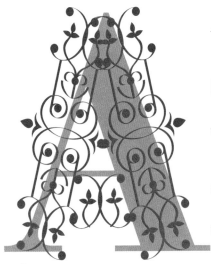fter the lords and nobles of Assisi were expelled and their towers were pulled down, a new revolutionary Council was elected by the people. The lords began to feel a bit queasy behind their fortressed castles and palaces surrounded by moats.

To be on the safe side, the aristocrats fled to Perugia, a town that had always been hostile to Assisi. To sleep completely soundly, they brought along their own private troops. As an added precaution they recruited mercenary soldiers as reinforcements. To be absolutely certain they were secure from the rabble, their soldiers hurled themselves and their arsenal at the rebels of Assisi. There was a great clash between the noble's army skilled in warcraft and the rabble of untrained men from Assisi, who were more suited to wave olive branches on Holy Easter than to pierce the enemies' bellies with swords and pikes. The outcome was a massacre.

"The lords had invaded and again taken possession of Assisi!"

Francis was among Assisi's fighters that day. He had only just recovered from the vertigo of the Great Bang: the dizzying blows he received pulling down the Mangia Tower. Half of the men from Assisi were slaughtered like lambs; the others were captured and taken to prison in Perugia. Francis was among those rounded up and caged. For a whole year he remained locked up in Perugia's deep prison, suffering freezing cold in the winter, thirst and great heat in the summer. But his appearance was so mild and meek, none could fail to offer him help and protection.

Finally back in the air of freedom, Francis and his companions rushed home to their beloved Assisi, only to find themselves in total shock: the lords had invaded and again taken possession of Assisi. But their indignation was not yet complete. By dint of arms and threats, the Lords forced the rebels, the towers destroyers, to rebuild the towers, stone by stone.

Francis, whose health had buckled under the prison shackles, found himself hoisting granite boulders, chiseling, squaring them, and raising walls back into the sky. The poor man was so shook up and convulsed, after just two days hammering rocks, that his delicate hands, soft as a newborns, were crushed between the hammer and anvil of the blacksmith.

The wardens smirked at his piteous state: "We will not weep for you, you sly old fox! You've ruined your hands on purpose, to avoid raising the towers you tore down! Bend your back and put your shoulder to the wall!"

An old mason, whose own hands had been weathered by a lifetime of stone work, bound up Francis' fingers with bandages and then dipped his hands into a pot of eggs and wheat glue. The next day when he appeared at the site it seemed that Francis had put on a pair of gauntlets. After a week, Francis, the bricklayer had become so adept and quick at moving stones and fixing them in place on the wall, he looked like a juggling acrobat!

HOLY JESTER!

"We will not weep for you, you sly old fox! You've ruined your hands on purpose!"

The BATTLE AGAINST the CITIZENS of PERUGIA

FRANCIS MEETS

the

WOLF

in

GUBBIO

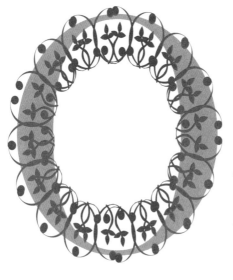ne day,
Francis is
on his way
to Gubbio,
to meet his
comrades,
when he hears some
peasants screaming...

"Help! God save us! The great Butcher is at our throats! Run for your lives!"

"What's happening? Who is after you?"

"The Wolf from Gubbio! A monster!"

"A lion!"

"A lion! Please! There are no lions in these parts. Don't exaggerate!

"His face looks like a crocodile! He opens his jaws this wide ready to snap you in two."

"I've seen him tear a lamb apart with a single bite!"

"I saw him pick up a dog with his jaws and chop up the poor mutt like sausage meat."

"When he shows you his fangs and his tremendous eyes, it curdles your blood!"

"Get a hold of yourselves, my friends. I don't see anything."

"Over there, Francis, look: he's bounding down across the valley!"

"But he's quite small!"

"From here he's quite small. Believe me, it is a matter of perspective. Wait till he gets nearer. You'll see."

"Well, I'd like to go and meet him."

But Francis' brothers hold him back: "Dear Francis, please, brother, calm down. You've gone crazy again. First you embrace the lepers, then you strip off naked in the church and now you want to talk to wolves! Why don't you just write the Wolf a letter instead?"

"The Wolf will chomp Francis to bits in two seconds flat."

"No, I want to speak to him personally!"

Francis breaks away and heads down the hill into the valley.

Peasants, shepherds, women, children—everybody heading to the ridge, to witness the grand confrontation as if they were in an amphitheater:

"This should be good!"

"Won't see a match like this again in my lifetime."

"Show won't last long, though. The Wolf will chomp Francis to bits in two seconds flat."

Francis strides down the slope and from around the bend ahead of him, the wolf appears again.

"Bah, there's nothing to be frightened of;

he looks rather puny!" Francis smiled.

"Stand back, Francis. We told you its a question of perspective! Wait till he reaches you!" the peasants warn him from above.

The wolf leaps forward closer and closer ... and finally when they are six steps from each other, Francis exclaims:

"What a gigantic beast! Good heavens, you are not a mountain lion! You are a mountain! And what fangs! Now I wish I had written that letter after all and said ciao!"

At the top of the ridge men are taking bets: 'Now watch, my money says the wolf will devour him in one gulp!'

"I say two gulps!"

"I say three!"

The wolf approaches Francis, step by step. The entire population of Gubbio holds its breath. Men and women cross themselves. Girls close their eyes. When there is no sound of gnashing teeth or limbs being torn from their sockets, the girls open their eyes, and this is what they see: When he's right in front of Francis, the wolf slowly crouches down on his paws, like a farm dog, bends his head and rests his jaws between Francis' feet.

The spectators think they have seen the greatest marvel until Francis begins to speak to the wolf:

"Now then, dear Wolf, what's the matter with you? Eh? Do you think that these are nice things to do? Are you a credit to the Heavenly Father's creation? Answer me!"

41

The peasants above are shouting: "Hey, speak up! We can't hear a damned thing!"

"Oh, butt out! This is a private conversation!"

Turning back to the wolf: "Now then, dear Wolf, never mind them. Strictly entre nous, would you like to tell me what's got into your head? You go around tearing up dogs and sheep. But do you even taste them? No, you don't! It's just for the pleasure of tearing out their innards, of striking terror, eh? Isn't that it? Come on, speak up, I am talking to you."

"AHOOOO! AMAHOOGA ... Oh well, I na, give, up, or scac hotorn, lave ne ..."

"Hey, you, Wolf, don't play beastly games with me! Speak properly!"

"Oh, yes, it's true, what's the point of denying it? I like biting, jumping on sheep, tearing away their innards and strewing them all around... I quite love seeing people running away and screaming in terror... Ha, ha, ha!"

"And do you think this is nice ... eh? Am I supposed to be impressed?"

"What else can I do? That's my nature. It's my natural behavior! Blame Nature!"

"Oh, that's a ripe old excuse! Nature! Did you think that ditty up all by yourself? Bravo! You are a bit of jester yourself. Now it is all nature's fault! If someone is born with the nature of a thief, he can steal! An arsonist can burn down the town. Slaughtering, lying, killing, it is all Nature's fault! And woe betide the man who raises his arm against a curse of Nature? And what about those poor souls who are lacking in nature—the poor, the ragged, the weak—blows raining on their heads, kicks up their asses and spit in their eyes! This is what they deserve! On your knees, Miscreant bend your head! ... No, no, my dear wolf! It's not honest!"

"Well, what's it got to do with me? Blame the Eternal Father! He made me this way."

"Did the Eternal Father decree for you to lead a cursed life? Or a blessed one? Answer me!"

"Now that you put it that way, you've got a point there, Francis; it really is a dog's life, looking at it from a wolf's point of view. I really would like to live like a good little gentle beast. Don't think I haven't given goodness a whirl. But it was no good. There was the time I tried to become a vegetarian, eating vegetables and roots. But after a week I had such terrible runs! I

43

FRANCIS MEETS the WOLF in GUBBIO

ran and ran all over the place. But you know, I really would like to be good. If you help me, Francis, I am ready to change my life!"

"You are? Are you truly prepared to do so? Swear on it! Are you going to swear?"

"Yes, I do. I swear!"

"Hey, you, up there, peasants, brothers! The wolf has pledged to change his life. He is going to be good. But you must help him. He cannot do it alone. Take him with you into your community. You only need to feed him. Throw him the leftovers, the same that you give to your dogs: the wolf eats, the dogs eat and everyone is at peace! What do you say?"

"Fine, but what are we going to get out of it?"

"For a start he will not maul you! He will not tear you limb for limb. How's that for a nice little quid pro quo? Then, once he's developed a decent reputation, he can guard you from the other wolves and even from the brigands and murderers who are always after you. Don't worry; he will earn his keep."

"So, dear wolf, do you agree? Are we going to enter into this contract? Don't make me cut a poor figure in front of this flock. And you, peasants, are you convinced? Shall we go ahead with this deal? Well then!

I'm coming up to introduce you: this, my friends, is my friend, the Wolf. Dear Wolf, I'm pleased to be able to present to you, your new friends, the Peasants. Aren't you going to shake hands on it? No, perhaps there's no need for this ritual at the outset. Go on then, off you go."

They form a procession: the wolf in the middle, the peasants and the women around him, all walking in harmony at the same pace.

"Be careful," Francis calls after them, "don't step on his toes! Don't tempt his Nature to spring out and savage you!"

The kids hang back at the rear of the line. Everyone disappears over the ridge, leaving Francis and his brothers alone.

"Well, this wolf matter is settled! But the day is not done. Let's start out for the quarry in Stroppiana to get our stones!"

Francis and his brothers set off up the mountain and reach the quarry the following day. The quarrymen, who dig out the marble slabs, immediately recognize Francis. After all, he is a well known bricklayer by now:

"Hey, Francis, long time we don't see you! They say now you have been repairing churches! How's it going?"

"It was going all right until we ran out of stones ... I need three or four cartfuls!'

"I am sorry, Francis, but unfortunately nobody can take away stones, slabs or blocks. Not anymore."

"Why not? Doesn't the quarry belong to the town? And doesn't the town belong to the people? And aren't we the people?"

"Very true. Until recently."

"What happened?"

"The monk—you know, the Celestian, from Civitella, where the monastery was hit by an earthquake? So they figured this was a good time to hit the Pope up for some stuff. So they went to the Pope: "Holy Father, a wall of our monastery has collapsed in the terrible earthquake. We need to dig out stones from the Stroppiana quarry. Won't you please give us the exclusive privilege to take away stones? Just for one week so we can get back on our feet?"

"For a week? All right," said the Pope, "if it's only for a week, go fix your wall. I give you this privilege."

On their way back home, the Pope dies and the monks changed their story: "The quarry is ours. The Pope gave us the privilege in perpetuity."

Francis becomes red, filled with anger. "Perpetuity is a long time. Those wicked monks, imagine cheating the Pope! On his deathbed no less! I am going to give these Celestian monks a piece of my mind. Make way!"

Francis' companions try to hold him back.

"Francis, calm down! Yesterday morning you worked in the fields, then you converted the wolf. Then we hiked to Stroppiana. Now you want to take on the Celestian monks! Relax! Let it drop! We'll get stones someplace else."

"Stones don't just grow on trees you know?"

"Watch out, Francis, these monks are pretty cocky!"

"They don't listen to reason like the wolf."

"And the prior, when he sees you arriving in rags looking like a beggar, he will let loose the fearful hounds on you!"

※

"Dogs, against me? What can dogs do to me? To one who talks to the wolves! Listen: if you are afraid, I'll go to the monastery alone. Wait for me here, at Stroppiana. We shall take our stones home yet."

So Francis goes it alone. He arrives at the monastery in the middle of the night. He takes hold of the doorknocker, lifts it up, and bangs it on the door: BODONG!

No answer. Again he lifts up the doorknocker: BODONG!

"Owwww!!! Ooouch!" He forgot to take his hand away!

When he screams, the guardian comes out onto the highest arcade.

"Who is shouting at this time of the night?"

"It's me, Francis. I need ..."

"I know what you need, ragged as you are: Food! You are all looking for food! I'm sorry, it's too late: No bread. Come back tomorrow!"

"No, no, please! I don't want bread, but stones!"

"Stones? Have you come at this hour of the night to play a practical joke? Get lost! Or I'll give you stones on your head!"

"No, sorry, I won't go away! I need to speak personally to the Prior!"

Francis pushes against the door with his shoulder and when it gives way, he slips into the portico shouting:

"Prior, Father Prior!"

On the tallest tower appears the Head Monk. "Who is it? Who's calling me at this hour?"

"It's me, Francis! I need to get stones from the quarry!"

"Ah, I know you, you are the madcap from Assisi! You strip naked in the church, you steal money from your father and give it to tramps like yourself! I know you! You embrace lepers! You are diseased! Get out,

49

FRANCIS MEETS the WOLF in GUBBIO

or I'll set the hounds on you!"

"Sorry, but I cannot go away. It was the Lord Jesus Christ in person who ordered me: "Go and save my church!" His voice echoed around the stone walls.

"Set the hounds on him!' ordered the Prior.

Two servants appear, dragged in by two wild beasts. Francis tries to turn but the dogs are already upon him. They seize his buttocks—those tiny, skinny buttocks of his—"Oihoihh! Ooouuch," he shouts as they begin savaging him.

"Maybe I should have come at a more civilized hour," he thought.

Suddenly, Francis sees out of the corner of his eye, a black shadow out of nowhere that pounces on the mastiffs followed by a wild roaring: 'Ohahooheeehah!"

Soon the two mastiffs flee, whimpering: "Kaiiikaiiiikaiikaiiii!!!"

"But what's this black shadow? Ho! Is it you, the Wolf from Gubbio?"

"Yes, it is me!"

"And what are you doing around in these parts, dear Wolf?"

"Oh, I was just passing by and I recognized your voice screaming and I came in to give the hounds a good bite—for old time's sake!"

"Well done! You did very well; I was having some problems with those animals. Listen to me, dear wolf: it might be best if we get out of here immediately because the Prior is even more vicious than his dogs. Let's go!"

And off they go up the slope.

"Tell me, dear Wolf, didn't you like it at Gubbio, with all those peasants feeding you?"

"Oh, yes Francis, I did. At first it was great: they treated me really well, giving me excellent scraps, petting, caressing me; they even deloused me! I never once took a bite out of any one. Then—and I don't know how it happened—they began to be disrespectful. They spat on me, they kicked me; not to mention the food—slop! vomit!—even the pigs wouldn't touch it! The kids threw stones at me ... While I was sleeping, they tied some straw to my tail and set it on fire! Look, it's all singed! What a tail! I am so ashamed that when I meet someone, I hide it between my legs! In the end I ran away! You know, Francis, I understood one thing: if someone is born a wolf, he must remain a wolf; because if you forget to bite, and grind your teeth, and terrorize the neighborhood with your voice ... nobody respects you: they take you for a fool and they spit on you!"

"Yeah, you're darned right, Wolf. It was my fault. I was arrogant! It was not Nature's fault. It was my fault. I tried to turn animals into good men. I should have tried to turn men into good animals!"

FRANCIS MEETS the WOLF in GUBBIO

IV

The

TIRADE

of

FRANCIS

at

BOLOGNA
15th AUGUST 1222

or 30 years, Bologna has been at war with the neighboring city of Imola. Now, in desperation, the Franciscan brothers of the city have asked Francis to come and try to stop the bloodshed. Francis addresses the crowd...

"Neapolitans! I embrace you! Oh, what gusto, what joy it is for me to be here with you, Neapolitans! Marvelous armed men you are! You attack like ferocious beasts in combat. And how tough you are! When you go to war, to battle, you butcher and kill, shouting on horse-back: "Murder, quarter, spear, behead! Bravo! Well done!" Neapolitans, good people, courageous, hearty ... What? You are not Neapolitans? Where are you from? From the city of Bologna?! All of you? The women too? And what are you doing here in Naples, you of Bologna? Are you just passing through? What a coincidence, eh? You are heading to the Holy Land? Of course, you are boarding the ship? No ... ? We are not in Naples?! Where are we? Bologna?

"This is the city of Bologna?!

"Are you sure? Oh God! ... I am staggered!

So that explains why I didn't see the volcano! Where oh where did Vesuvius go! Come to think of it I was also thinking to myself: 'Where did the sea go? Didn't there used to be quite a big ocean nearby?' Ha, ha, but we are in Bologna! Ha, ha, ha. This is really funny! ... What a calamity! Ah, you're right! It's the day after tomorrow that I have to go to Naples! ... I got it wrong! I am so confused!

   "I have been practicing the dialect with a friar in my monastery from Naples: all day long I talked to him in the Neapolitan dialect. I kept on asking him:

   "Talk to me in your language! I want to learn this fanciful, extravagant language. Speak to me, immerse me, drown me in Neapolitan so that when I arrive in Naples I'll make them stand there open-mouthed." Ha, ha, ha, and all the Neapolitans gaping in amazement:

   'Look at him, Francis is speaking like a native, Francis the Neapolitan!'

   "But, what a fool, I have made a colossal mistake! I was all ready to speak Neapolitan, but now I'm here in Bologna ... I don't speak the Bolognese dialect, not a syllable. It's a hard language, it's so difficult to pronounce. And now what? This is quite a pickle I find myself in. If we'd had a friar from Bologna, that would be a different story.

"Please, lend me a hand! Try to content yourself with the Neapolitan dialect ... pretend that you understand it. Act like you catch every word and even when you don't understand it, pretend you do! Will you? Is that too much to ask? Thank you, thank you! How gentle and generous you are! I love you, I kiss each one of you."

✠

"Bolognese! What lovely people you are! Bursting, overflowing with fierce courage, you fight, you battle, you slaughter each other, crazy with ecstasy!"

"Where did the sea go? Didn't there used to be quite a big ocean nearby?"

The TIRADE of FRANCIS at BOLOGNA

Fire! A blaze!
Burn, stick and sink!
Spear a horse with the lance!
Slashing the paunches,
Squashing the bellies!
With a sword, with a lance,
With a mace, with a pike!
The axe is coming down,
Deep is the wound!
Trucca, tigna, beffa, soffia, zurra, cacchia,
ricacchia—TIEH!!!

"Bolognese!
"How nice you are! Such a long time you
have been at war against the people of
Imola, that infamous, ugly race! Horrible
beasts, animals they are! So rightly and
properly you crush them, crush and burn!
Crush and burn! Bravo!
"What a brawl! What a battle!
"You set half of their city on fire and in
revenge they went for your women. I saw
one soldier dragging a woman: 'Come
up here!' 'Let me go, let me go, you pig!'
He dragged her and her kid up the tower.
Her little child was screaming and yelling,
'Momma! Momma!' 'Oh, so you want to see
your Momma, do you? Here you go! Go to
Momma!'
SPLAT SPLAT!

"Once at night time—oh, this was magnificent—you rode out with the cavalry and tied long ropes to the door of the main entrance to Imola, unhinged the door and pulled it down. Then—and this was brilliant— you took it to Bologna and set it up in your biggest square as a monument! And those stinkers, those bastards from Imola, with the wind blowing through the city day and night, they all caught a cold, ha ha ha, ha ha! Well done, Bolognese, well done!

"And what then? Some rest? A bit of peace? Nonsense! You turned against the Emperor, Frederick I, Barbarossa, the Red Beard, that animal of a man who had come to suck the blood of the Lombards—your blood—and wrench taxes and levies and fees out of you. You chased him and his army out of the region, shouting: 'We've had it with you fattening yourself on our meat! Thief!' And by the river Tanaro, close to the city of Parma, you destroyed his entire army, you unhorsed him! And he, the Emperor—that Kraut—hid himself under his horse, pretending to be dead. Bravo! Bravo! Bolognese, well done!

"Oh, how lucky they are, pillaging, killing, making off with women!"

"And what then? A bit of peace, some rest? No. Never! The Pope came, Innocent the Third, nicknamed "The Warrior." Raging at the Cathars—those bloody heretics going round proclaiming: 'That one is not the Pope, he's the Antichrist! He only thinks about women, having castles, everybody else's land! He's the Antipope!'

"They should never have said that! For shame! Pope Innocent the Third had all the saints spinning around his head; he mounted a horse, charged with a spear and dragged the French army against the Albigensians. And you Bolognese, along with the French, you mounted your horses too and rode behind him, shouting and chanting and hacking and slashing:

'Oh oh oh, domine noster—ZLONK!!!
Christum saeculorum—WHACK!
Sine die nobis miserere—POW!
Ahha Alleluja!
Domine Domine!
Aaamen!'

"Those poor bastards who didn't go to battle lamented: 'Oh, how lucky they are, pillaging, killing, making off with women! And we, what are we louts doing? Scratching our bellies?'

61

The TIRADE of FRANCIS at BOLOGNA

"But not to fear for those who stayed behind the action was also heating up. The Lords of Bologna began to snap and snark at each other—battle cries of 'Ayee!' went up—The Bonzoni against the Albergitti! The Camarini against the Zamborghi!—'Ayee!'— whole streets were burned down, women and children murdered ... In one short week 450 dead! All Bolognese! A record that will stand for all eternity. Such satisfaction, slaughtering within the family! Such beauty, all these funerals parading through the town—one funeral coming down from that road, another funeral coming from the square. A grand festival where everybody knew each other, they were waving: 'Oh, look, I killed that one. Of course, he killed my son.'

"Exult! Cheer! Hoooray! Those who went to fight in Provence are coming back ... No, not all of them, because many have been killed. Naturally, only those who survived are coming back. But to watch them all marching proudly—singing with their flags to the wind and the trumpets, the drumming—in such martial order, all strutting, like this ... No, no, not quite like that, because many of them were lame—one with a blind eye, another one with a foot chopped off, that one without a hand—but so proud they were! All lopsided marching with their chests puffed out but leaning a bit to one side: crooked—but, my God, so proud!

"And what then, a bit of peace, some rest? No! Never! 'Alarum, alarum, alarum!' What's happened? The Muslims have robbed the Holy Sepulchre, the hallowed grave is hollow! Innocent the Third calls out to Christians everywhere: French, German and English, even the Danish. They marched through our country, to the port of Brindisi, crossed the Mediterranean Sea, arrived in the Palestinian Land with arrows, shields,

horses ... Holy massacre! Six thousand killed; dead! Six thousand new graves ... to liberate one empty grave!

"And when they came back from the Holy Land—the few that made it back—so many more were buried there—they were so proud! They were boasting, showing off and crying out: 'I was there on the battlefield! I fought for my country, for my religion and for the flag. I sacrificed myself!'

"'Ah hah—but where, please, is the mark of war? You must show us the wound, the gash! It is our holy right to see the wound. Look at him, he claims to come back from such bloodshed and not a scratch on him, nothing. Hey, how did that happen?'

'Hey, buddy, you look better now than when you left? Hey, how did that happen?'

'Oh, well, I was lucky.' 'Lucky? Do me a favor! You've been in a brothel with the whores!'

"But if someone's sacrifice is marked—then hooraaaay!

"'My hand? You can see: it's not there! The other hand? I haven't got one.'

"'Very well, you pass muster! Bravo! Indeed you have been at war! You are a hero! You are a patriot! Let me shake your hand!'

"'But I don't have a hand! Take my foot!'

"Hey, women ... females ... who's crying? Why are you crying? What? You lost your husband?! Where, in Provence? And you? You lost your son? Where, in Palestine? "You, your father? So sorry. And you, you lost your lover! I am so sad for you. Ah, I can see so many mothers in grief, so many widows! But you must be immensely proud of your

widowhood! Yes! You gave your sons, your men, for your country. So honored you look! So proud ... !

"No? You are not proud?!

"Woman, what are you saying to me?! You would prefer to have your son embrace you, alive? ... And you, your husband's head on your bosom? You, your father, your brother? You don't care about the glory and the honor?! Whaat! You too?

"All of you!?

"Oh God! The shame! Disgrace!

"The shame! Catastrophe!"

"I hope this doesn't mean you won't listen to any more holy speeches from our notables. What's that? You would like to think and to reason with your own brain, with your own head! This is very dangerous! People could get hurt!

"I can already imagine in a day or two: you will be standing in front of the town hall, asking the Mayor to sign a peace treaty with all our enemies and to impose a perpetual truce even on the families of Bologna!

'Go! Go!'

'What a catastrophe!'

"I can see you now reaching for Peace...
what a lovely word peeeace is! You fill your
mouth with it: Peeeaacce ..."

(singing)

The sun is rising,
Beautiful and free,
Then it blazes up,
High in the sky,
Till it goes down, and
The moon comes out,
Another day is gone.
The sun is out again,
It will last
Till the stars reappear
in the sky.
The peasant is digging,
Then he sows the wheat.
The earth is thirsty,
The wheat can't grow.
Hope it's gonna rain,
Rain, rain, rain ...
Tink ... tink ... tink ...
Hey, slow down!
I said rain,
This is a storm !
The sun is rising again,

The seeds are sprouting,
The girl is in love,
And she gets pregnant ...
Quick, quick, a marriage,
Before the baby is born!
In the church,
Din don dun,
The bell is rang,
Din don dun.
Everybody
Dance and sing,
Drink and chant!
The sun is rising
The wheat's growing,
The child is getting taller,
Hope he won't go to war.
The sun is rising ...
Another day is gone,
Peace, peace, peace ...
Peace, peace, peace ...

Three days later, the people of Bologna marched to the town hall and demanded the Mayor and the notables sign a peace treaty with the town of Imola. Known as the Concilium Pacis, it is on display in the Museum of Bologna today.

The TIRADE of FRANCIS at BOLOGNA

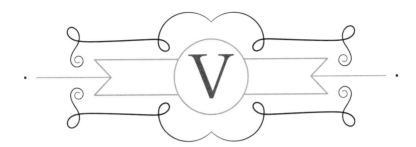

FRANCIS

the

HOLY

JESTER

and the

CHICKEN

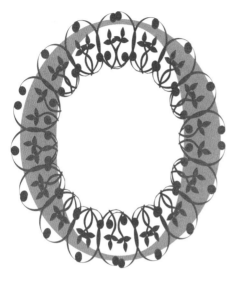ne day in the Assisi town square, people were stunned by a deafening noise. On the flight of steps of the Roman temple, a nutcase, an oddball, covered in rags and leaves, appeared, blowing a trumpet with one hand and beating a drum with the other.

Tethered to him by a long chain was a naked man with his crown jewels fluttering in the wind.

"Who is this shameless fellow showing us his merchandise?" an old woman asks.

"It is Francis, Bernardone's son. Who else?"

"Yes, that one, the naked guy in chains."

"The same fool who stripped off inside the cathedral?!"

"Can there be two such giddy goats? Stripping off in public, it's a fixation with him!

"Quiet! The oddball is about to speak!"

Everyone falls silent as Francis speaks in a loud voice:

"You see? People, it's me that ordered my brother in Christ to chain me up and drag me naked through the streets. To crown me on the head with his baton. Go on, friar, beat me! Every blow is a blessing!"

The friar deals Francis a severe blow.

"Ayeee, what a blow! Please, brother, not so hard; don't go overboard!"

"Behold, I am the worst of sinners: last night I proved it once and for all: for last night, I ... I ... ate a whole chicken, the whole fat and juicy chicken. I discovered the poor innocent creature in my path still very much alive. Worse than a weasel I pounced on it. I grabbed it and I throttled it. I knew very well that this big, fat, juicy chicken belonged to a peasant who lives just two steps away! But that did not stop me! I played dumb and tucked the bird under my shirt and went running by leaps and bounds down the road. The animal, at every step, was tearing at my stomach with its claws to escape. I tightened my grip under its neck, and soon its claws stopped tearing at me. I had killed it. Brothers and Sisters, I stand before you a chicken thief, a murderer, and a butcher.

"First I plucked it, then I greedily opened its stomach ... I filled it with the most fragrant herbs. Ah, the rosemary and sage. I skewered the creature on a stick and gently, slowly I roasted it. Ah, the tasty fragrance, the wonderful aroma of that holy creature's flesh!"

HOLY JESTER!

"Beat me, brother, beat me! For I am the worst sinner of all time! Am I not the hypocrite who goes around preaching the blessedness of poverty: 'Blissful and joyful are those as poor as a church mouse, who are content with the wild herbs and berries on the side of the road and then chant glory to the Lord.' Who speaks these words? It is I, Francis, the holy hypocrite who goes around glorifying: 'Blessed are the birds that peck worms and gnats, and are content.'

"But my sins do not stop there, brothers and sisters. I succulate the chicken's wings and its tender legs ... I lick my hands ... I bite its luscious behind, 'the parson's nose', the best part. For shame, but it is a delicacy!

"You see before you a liar, an imposter, and a hypocrite! There is no one in the world worse than me!

The townspeople, who at first were amused and entertained, now grew serious, and Francis again orders:

"Brother of mine, come, bring down your cudgel!"

The friar hits him so hard that Francis' nose starts bleeding.

FRANCIS the HOLY JESTER and the CHICKEN

"Stop it, my son!" a woman shouts. "We all are sinners. Look at me: I too have grasped a chicken to eat."

"Yes," says Francis, "but then you do not go around promising heaven to those who fast out of devotion. You do not go around convincing desperate souls that simply breathing fresh air is enough to obtain bliss and holiness. You do not sprinkle yourself with holy water to merit the company of the angels! Beat me friar, me, this rotter who devours roast chickens and dupes his brethren about his true nature. It's you who are the chickens, you who have confidence in me! Move along, do not stand there dumbfounded, gaping. Spit in my face ... Pick up this stone and hurl it at me, for I am the damned liar!"

"What a crafty trickster!" a listener bursts out. "Get it? He's the living allegory. It's all an act. Don't you see? That man comes here buck naked, gets himself beaten up with a stick for swiping a chicken. But he's really getting at those arrogant noble bastards who're up to much worse schemes devouring our goods and livelihoods--none of whom show a whit of repentance or remorse! This Francis is a great jester!"

Everyone shouts, "Bravo!" and goes wild with applause. Then, at his feet, some people leave melons, oranges, sweet cakes, a sackful of wheat, a bucket of mushrooms, three big loaves of bread and a live chicken.

Francis watches the townspeople trail away and, still tied to the chains, blubbering, he cries

"Oh, Lord, how difficult it is to denounce oneself as sinner!"

FRANCIS the HOLY JESTER and the CHICKEN

VI

FRANCIS CALLS

on the

POPE

rancis once again is striding along the road to Gubbio. He's walking through the village of Beast, near Bastard, when all of a sudden he hears voices calling out his name...

"Hey! Francis!" three young men run up to him smiling. "How wonderful we have found you!"

"Greetings. But I'm quite late ..."

"We were searching everywhere for you!'

"What for?"

"The best reason—a wedding!"

"A great pal of ours is getting hitched to a girl so sweet that she looks like spring."

"How impossibly young they are! You should see them!"

"You must come, Francis, and greet them and cheer the feast with one of your stories from the Gospel. What a blessing that would be at the festivities."

"I am very sorry. I'm so late already. My companions are waiting. Send the couple my blessing."

"One story! Come on, Francis, a five minute detour, tops. Please!"

"I wish I could, but I can't. I've got to go."
"One glass of wine with us is too much?"
"Oh, well! If it's one glass of wine..."

❧

They arrive at the marriage feast. The guests greet and embrace him: 'Francis, how good to see you, sit down!"

"We are truly honored."

"Have a drop of wine, have a nice piece of roast! Eat!"

Everybody drinks a toast to the bride, who is crying with joy. Her mother is crying. In a moment all the women are crying!

The father's voice cries out: "If we carry on like this, we'll flood the whole table with tears. Come on, Francis, put an end to all this whining, tell us a story!"

Francis stands up and begins: "All right, I will try to tell you a story, and rightly from the Gospel. And since this is a wedding, I will tell you the tale of the Wedding at Cana...

"The situation was just as it is here: the bride was crying, the mother weeping, the father grumbling, and none of the guests were seated at the table.

"Someone asks in panic: 'What's going on? Has the groom run away?'

'No, no, the groom is swearing like a trooper!'

'Didn't the priest show up?'

'Much much worse. There's been the most

horrible stroke of fate...'

'No, don't tell me!'

'Yes, verily I say unto thee: they've run out of wine!'

'Oh, dear God, not that!'

'A bride wet with wine is a lucky bride ...'

'But wet with water is a curse, a misfortune, a danger to flee!'

"At that moment another guest, a latecomer, a young man arrived with his mother on his arm. His name was Jesus. But he also went by his nickname, Christ. His

FRANCIS CALLS on the POPE

mother was well known to the guests as a wonderful woman known as The Madonna.

"The bride's father held up the empty wine jug to The Madonna and said:

'Madonna, dear, we are mortified but we have no wine to offer. I don't know how it happened! This family must be cursed. We've run out of wine on my daughter's wedding day!'

'Run out of wine? So soon? Why have you bought so little?'

'So little? Oh, Madonna, we bought enough wine for three weddings but these people don't drink wine; they guzzle it! Please, Madonna, help us!'

'But I don't know anything about wine! You should ask my son Jesus. He knows a quite bit about wine.'

"As soon as the bride's father approached him, Jesus said:

'Yes, yes, I've heard you are running out of wine, but 'wine miracles' are not my specialty.'

'Well, can we try one as an experiment?'

'Yes, we can try. I can't guarantee anything, but sure, we can try. All right, have you got some water? If you have also run out of water, then we are sunk.'

'Water? We've got all the water you like. Didn't you see, when you came to the house, just in front of the door? There are seven vessels of water. As you know, we not only wash our hands before the feast, but also our feet. 'Clean feet before the feast refreshes brain and spirit.' There are even some louts that step straight into the bucket with their shoes on!'

'All right! Bring me the water, please.'

'But, Jesus, you're not going to make wine with that water, are you? It has such an unpleasant smell!'

'Excuse me, dear Lady, but when you make wine what do you do?'

'We take the grapes ...'

'And after?'

'We put the grapes into a vat ...'

'And after?'

'We climb into the vat and tread the grapes with our feet ...'

'So, feet before or feet afterwards—it's the same thing, no?'

'... Oh, yes, indeed I didn't think about it like that.'

"We've run out of wine on my daughter's wedding day!"

"At this point the young man whose other alias was the Messiah, raises his right hand to the sky, then he takes the fingers one by one and pulls and pops them. Then he holds up three fingers—with the other two held tight against the palm—and makes a sign over the water which the guests don't understand: it's the sign of the cross, but nobody understands it because they don't know that

Jesus will end up nailed to the cross. Then the water in the vessels begins to quiver ... it changes color ... until it becomes red ... it boils ... and, as clouds of pink vapor rise from the bottom, the smell of crushed grapes spreads all around the hillside! Someone staggers by, already drunk. Someone who is dying of thirst picks up a small mug and dips it into this new wine.

'Stop it, for Christ's sake!" says Jesus 'It's still hot, you'll burn yourself. Let it cool down a little! Then we'll test it. Remember, this is an experiment.'

"With the very first sip, everybody knew: 'What wine!'

'Ye gods, blessed in purgatory!'

'Mellow, a little bitter in the middle, a little salty at the back...'

'A bit sharp—at least three years old, a golden vintage!'

"Jesus climbs up onto a table and begins pouring wine for everybody: 'Drink, good people, be happy, be mirthful, do not wait for heaven tomorrow! Today, here, on earth, this is heaven!'

"Then he meets his mother's eyes: 'Forgive me mother, I am a little drunk ...'

"Everybody raises his cup: 'Bravo, Jesus!'

'Bravo Jesus! Jesus, you are divine! Or perhaps we should we say 'di-wine!'"

A priest claps and laughs for joy: "Francis, how wonderful you are, how good you are at telling stories! I have never heard the Gospel told in such a fresh way. You are one funny guy! Did anybody ever tell you that? A genuine jester! But, excuse me, I have to ask you something ... I don't want to rain on your parade. Only to keep you from being struck by lightning .... Tell me, Francis, do you have permission to speak the Gospel in public? In the vulgar tongue too? In this way?"

"Why? Do I need permission?"

"Oh blissful innocence! But certainly, you need permission, for you are not a priest. It is a mortal sin! Beware Francis, when you go around preaching; be careful: Those Holy Inquisitors always sneaking around – they wouldn't think twice about burning you at the stake!"

"Holy Moses! What should I do?"

"Play it safe. Go and ask for permission from the Bishop, or the Cardinal, or—best of all—from the Pope."

"The Pope?"

"Yes, why not the Pope? If he gives the okay, nobody's going to give you any flack."

FRANCIS CALLS on the POPE

"Heavens! It never dawned on me ... Excuse me but I must tell my friars before it's too late. Thank you, thank you, dear priest. Goodbye, cheers to all of you, wish the newly-weds happiness and contentment. I must fly, my lovely friends. I kiss you dearly!"

⚜

Off Francis goes, sad and agitated, rushing so fast he nearly knocks over his fellow friars. When they see him they cry out:

"Francis, what's wrong?"

"Where were you?"

"You look like you've seen a ghost."

"Nothing. It's alright."

"Nothing? You're shaking!"

"Brothers, we can't go around speaking the Gospel anymore."

"What?"

"You're joking!"

"Why not?"

"We need permission."

"Permission?"

"Yes, permission. From now on, we can't just go around preaching the Love of Christ."

"We can't?"

"Not from the Gospel."

"How come?"

"The Holy Inquisition don't think twice about burning people at the stake. For just one misplaced Beatitude, they string you up."

"You got a plan, Francis? You've got that look in your eye!"

"We go to the Pope to ask for permission."

"To the Pope?"

"Yes, the Pope."

"The one in Rome?"

"How many other popes do you know?"

"Oh, I can see it all now: we go to Rome with our hands in our pockets and we announce ourselves: 'Hey, here we are, Pope, we've arrived. Now what about that permission?'"

"And why not? He's not going to eat us!"

"You never know ..."

So off they went, four friars and Francis, step by step, crossing the Tevere Valley, heading for Rome. After a week's walking, they enter Rome and ask:

"Excuse me, which way to the Pope?"

"Go down that road, turn left, then cross the bridge over the river, pass through that little valley, turn right, go up till you are in front of a big palace. Behind it, there is another big palace with a lot of windows. You can't miss it. Inside there, I don't know in which window, but there you will find the Pope."

"Thank you. You see, my brothers, all very straightforward!"

FRANCIS CALLS on the POPE

They go on walking, turning this way and that, and finally they arrive in front of the Palace.

"You see, boys, it's practically pre-ordained."

A row of guards blocks their way:

"Halt! Stop where you are. What do you want?"

"Good morning, my brothers! I am Francis, I have come from Assisi. I need to talk to the Pope."

"You think it's that easy to speak to the Pope!?"

"Well, we'd like to get back on the road as soon as possible."

"You want an audience with the Pope? Just like that?"

"First of all, you'll have to write a request, quite possibly in Latin."

"But I don't remember my Latin."

"Then write it as you like. The important thing is that you must be patient—very patient! Because patience is not only the virtue of the saints, but also of those tramps and wretches of the earth who own nothing, like you!"

"Oh, thank you very much! That was very instructive. You see boys, this is an educational field trip."

Francis scribbles a little note and hands it to the guard.

Francis and his companions sit down in the square and wait. And they wait. Evening comes, then night, then morning. Another day passes, and nobody calls them.

At this point Francis groans not without a hint of exasperation:

"This Pope is taking his sweet time ..."

Then he hits his forehead—

"Oh, how stupid, how boneheaded I am! Why didn't I think of it before! My dear friend, Giovanni lives right here in Rome!"

"Who is this Giovanni?"

"Colonna, Cardinal Colonna—he's the Pope's Counselor! He will get us in for sure. He is the answer to our prayers."

They ask around:

"Excuse me, please, where is the house of Cardinal Giovanni Colonna?"

"The Cardinal? Go down that road, turn right, go straight on for 200 meters and turn right again, go over a bridge and turn left, and there is a square, on the corner of that square there is a big palace with a lot of windows—I don't know in which window but that's where you'll find Colonna. You can't miss it."

FRANCIS CALLS on the POPE

They arrive in front of the Cardinal's house. They try to enter the Palace but the guards immediately stop the strange looking country friars: "Where do you think you are going?"

"To see Cardinal Colonna!"

"First you have to write a request, preferably—"

"In Latin, we know."

At that moment Cardinal Colonna getting dressed upstairs, glances out the window and what do his eyes reveal to him?

"Franciiis!! Can it be? Is that you?" he calls out of the window.

"Oh, Colonna! Colonna, what luck!"

"Stay there, Francis, don't move. I'm coming right down!"

Colonna trips so quickly down and around the winding staircase that when he reaches the bottom he has to make a half-turn back to stop himself spinning out of control.

"Oh Francis, what a blessing to embrace you! Let me take a look at you. You look like a thief, a brigand, you are so ragged. I will get you all new clothes."

"Our clothes are better than we deserve. But Colonna, I need your help: I came with my brothers to speak to the Pope."

"The Pope? This Pope?"

"Yes, why, do you have another one?"

"No, no, we have only this one, for now, but he's so haughty; so hoity-toity ..."

"Please, I need urgently to talk to him. Set

HOLY JESTER!

it up, Giovanni, and if we must we will make the ultimate sacrifice ... and bathe."

"All right, Francis, I'll see what I can do. But now, please, come, come inside; rest and be refreshed."

Then to the guards: "Take these dear friends of mine inside, give them the best of everything to eat and do everything in your power them to get to bathe. Whispering, he confides to his smartly attired guards: "They smell like the devil ... you can't go near them!"

Cardinal Colonna runs off to the Pope's palace, up the stairs and enters the grand hall. The Pope is sitting on his golden throne with a book in his hands, reading. "Oh, excuse me, dear Innocent ..." Colonna is very familiar with the Pope, and just calls him Innocent without the number.

"Colonna, tell me, what pressing matter presents itself at this hour?"

"A friend of mine, Francis, has just arrived from Assisi. He would like to talk to you."

"Francis, you say?"

"Yes, Francis."

"By chance, is he one of those who sat under the arcade from yesterday afternoon until this morning?"

"Yes, Francis is one of them."

"And, I ask you: this Francis, by chance, does he have a smile?"

FRANCIS CALLS on the POPE

"Yes, Francis has a smile."

"I do not like him."

"But why not? Francis is a fine man, a kind man!"

"Fiddlesticks! I do not like him. I do not like those who have a smile."

"But Francis is a good fellow, he's kind, he loves the Church ..."

"I don't care, I frown on those who smile! And I order all Christians to do the same. Do you remember that smiling one—Pietro Valdo was his name—the mad wretch from Provence? He too had the very same smile. Do you not remember the Waldensians, those laughing hyenas, those heretics? What a war they drove me to wage against them! I had to slaughter Christians like lambs at Holy Easter! I still have nightmares—I wake up with my hands covered with blood! I will not risk another war like that one right here in Rome! Send this smiling friar packing at once!"

"Hey, calm down, Innocent; don't get all worked up. All right, I'll send him away. Consider him gone. Good-bye. I salute you,

Innocent ... the Third!"

And off Colonna goes, running home, where Francis is eagerly waiting:

"I'm sorry, Francis, I don't know what to say... but the Pope has all the Bishops spinning around his head; he's having fits! Let's wait for a better day."

That evening Francis and the others cannot eat. They cannot sleep. On the other side of town the Pope also goes to bed without supper. The Pope too cannot sleep—he is shaking, sweating with a fever.

In the middle of the night the Pope has a terrifying nightmare: he is inside a big cathedral and all of a sudden the columns start trembling. The arches are breaking up: stones, bricks, glass shattering. Plaster everywhere; the floor is opening up—an earthquake! Just at that moment a little man appears, dressed in rags, and—ZAP!—with one hand, he stops a column from falling on his head, then—ZNEEP!—he raises a foot

FRANCIS CALLS on the POPE

and kicks another one back into place. Then the little man raises his arms, which stretch impossibly high and braces the main arch and, with one foot here, one foot there, he secures every part of the church structure.

"I frown on those who smile! And I order all Christians to do the same."

Silence!! Innocent wakes up in a sweat. He is trembling all over. He calls the chief guard:

"Go and get Colonna, my Counselor, bring Cardinal Colonna here, quickly! More quickly than quickly! Hurry up!"

And off goes the chief guard to Colonna's house and shouts: "Hello Colonna, it's me, the Pope's guard! Innocent wants to see you more quickly than quickly! Come at once!"

Colonna runs down the stairs and sets off towards the Pope's palace—Colonna, the Running Cardinal! When, breathless, he arrives, he asks the Pope:

"Innocent, what is happening at this hour?"

"Colonna, I had a horrible dream, a nightmare, but it was so real! I found myself under the main arch of the church and it was falling on me! The columns; the arches were coming down, and the floor was opening under my feet. Just then, a little man appeared. He stretched out his arms and legs and stopped the columns and the cupola from falling! He stopped everything from toppling on me!"

"Well then, it's all going to be fine!"

"No, Colonna, I know, a catastrophe is about to befall us! My bones are rattling."

"No, no, come on! Go back to bed. We'll be fine. But ... tell me, Innocent: what was he like? Who did he look like, the little man that you saw?"

"I don't remember, I was so upset!"

"Didn't you see his face? How was he dressed?"

"My mind is blank."

"But, listen, Innocent: by chance, did he have a smile?"

"You and your confounded smiles! But, yes ... now that you mention it, I remember: he wore a smile."

"Innocent, that was Francis! It was God himself that put this dream into your head: he wants you to meet Francis.'

"The suspicion did cross my mind ... Please, Colonna, go and fetch him, bring the fellow here immediately. I must speak to your little friend."

Colonna rushes back to his house and cries: "Francis, exult! The Pope—he wants to see

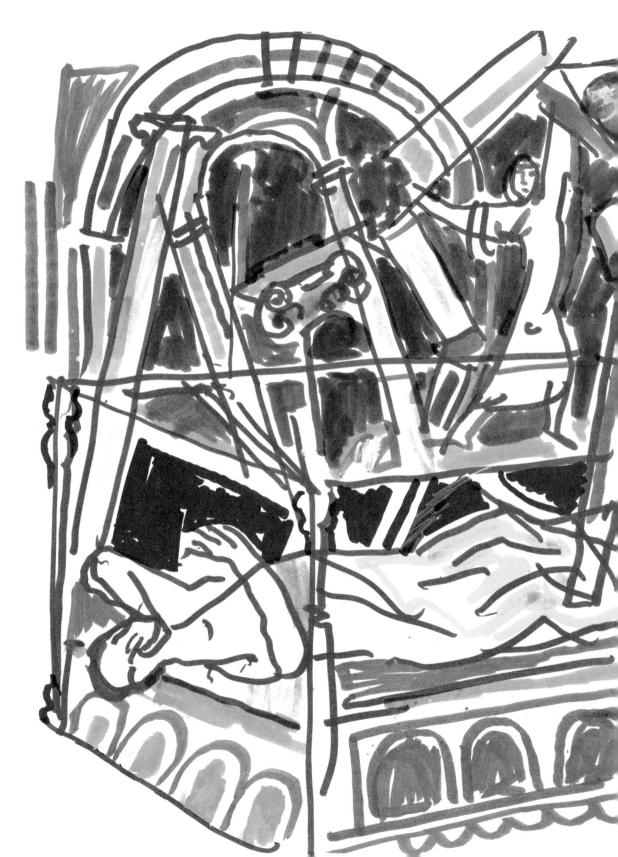

you. Let's go everybody, more quickly than quick, he's waiting. But please, Francis, put a lid on your smile."

When they arrive, the Pope points his finger at him: 'You are Francis?"

"It's me, Holy Father. I am Francis."

"Very well. Now, please, Colonna, leave Francis and me alone. You too, brothers, leave us."

✠

Now that they are alone the Pope continues: "Let me tell you, Francis, straightaway, whatever request you make of me, if it is in my power, I will grant it to you."

"Oh, Holy Father, how marvelous you are! You ask me to ask you, and, if you can, you are going to give to me what I ask for. Holy Father! I would like to share the Gospel with the people in the language of the streets with no fancy scholarly mumbo jumbo. I beg to tell the Gospel in the market square; in the streets; where people work; in the fields; in the taverns!"

"And in the churches? Never?"

"In the churches, forever, Holy Father. The Gospel is already in the churches. The priests are already there. We would just create confusion."

"You are right there, Francis. And what else do you ask? If it's within my power, I shall grant it to you."

97

"Oh, Holy Father, how magnificent you are! Then I beg for permission to build a Community that follows the Gospel as it is written; where everybody is equal and loves each other, and lives in poverty."

"Well, I like the idea. It's a good angle. Is that it?"

"Just about, Holy Father. Our first Rule will be that nobody shall own houses or land—or any possessions! We'll have no need for bags, or carts, or even pockets; for we'll have nothing to carry. We won't need homes. We will help the peasants in the fields to earn our living."

"That's a nice touch. I like it ... nobody needs goods because the Community doles them out. I follow you."

"Actually, there will be no community storehouse of goods. No house, no larder."

"But how will you survive? If there is a draught or a famine and there is no food left, what then?"

"We trust in Holy Providence! After all did He, our Lord Jesus, go around lugging shopping bags or pushing a cart? Did He carry a purse or asking for money? No, Holy Father, He did not!"

"Well, there you've got me; I forgot about Him. It's true about that one—a right mad specimen; but you can hardly run a whole community based on the habits of a crazy person! He and the other twelve like him;

98

quite insane, the whole bunch!

"But you forget one detail about him, my son. One small detail: that He, Jesus, happened to be the Son of God, and He was the Father too, and the Holy Spirit, all wrapped into one: Son of God, Father and Holy Spirit! You and your brothers unfortunately lack that facility."

"But, Holy Father ...."

"No one understood how He did it. For example, there was the time his disciples followed him around for days and days on end while he gave one revelation after another; needless to say the boys got very hungry. But you don't want to interrupt the Son of God on such a mundane matter. But when they settled in the mountains, and still everyone sat around him drinking the words from his lips, finally somebody beside him fainted onto the ground!

✠

"Jesus asked: 'What happened to this poor guy?'

'Well, Jesus, we haven't eaten all day.'

'So, what are we waiting for? Let's eat!'

'Yes, but, Jesus, we brought next to nothing.'

"When you're listening to the Son of God you don't think to pack a lunch. On top of which, the Palestinians were a bit disorganized to start with.

99

"But Jesus was not put off: 'Not even a crust of bread?'

'Wait, I have a small loaf of stale bread! But it's not much ...'

'Please, give it to me."

"Jesus broke it into pieces and put it in a basket.

'Not a scrap of cheese; dry meat; salami?'

'All the scraps are gone, Jesus.'

"Then, from the far end of the group, a voice rang out loud:

'I have a fish!'

"A cascade of sandwiches sailed down from the heavens - everything held in place with a toothpick!"

"Can you imagine someone up a mountain for three days with a fish in his pocket?

"Jesus took the three-day-old fish, broke it into small pieces, and threw it into the basket. Then he lifted up the basket, shook it and tossed everything up in the air.

"A cascade of sandwiches sailed down from the heavens! Slices of bread filled with fish wrapped with salad, the fish without any bones and everything held in place with a toothpick!

HOLY JESTER!

'Hurrah, hurrah, bravo Jesus!'"

"Everybody ate with great gusto and joy.
'What a meal! What a feast!'

'Jesus, surely, this is the most delicious religion ever!'

At this point in the Pope's parable, Francis bursts out laughing: "Ha, ha! Holy Father, you are the real jester, you are the storyteller, not me! Now I see, Holy Father. I get it. You mean that, since not one of us is able to perform miracles, there's no point in trying to start this Community. Let's leave it! It's not going to work. It's impractical."

"Wait, Francis, wait! Don't be so narrow-minded! I didn't take you for such a square. Aren't you forgetting the dialectic?"

"I don't understand, Holy Father. What do you mean?"

"Oh, my dear Francis, look at you: always wearing a smile, so charming that when you meet someone he will say: 'Look here Francis, I have so many cows, here, Francis, take this heifer, it's for you and your friends.'

"And you, Francis, can take the heifer and put it with your provisions! Along comes another one: 'Here, Francis, I have so many houses! Take one for yourself, Francis. Keep this house for you and your friends.'

"And there is someone else that says: 'Here, Francis, I have a lot of money, it's falling out of my pockets. Take this money, Francis, for you and your companions.' "And you,

FRANCIS CALLS on the POPE

Francis, can take the money! After all, where does the word 'Providence' come from? 'Providence'—from provisions! You make provisions for them; they make provisions for you."

✠

"Sorry," says Francis, "this dialectic—the give and the take—it is not possible. You see, Holy Father, when you take goods and store them, and then distribute them to the poor or to those in need; that is the greatest power of all—greater, even, than the power of the Emperor! The power of Charity! It's like this, Holy Father: you are poor? Here, take this heifer, it's for you, take it home. And you, too, are poor: this house is for you, take it. And you, here, take this money! And you? No, not you! I know that you're a poor man but I don't like you and I won't give you anything. It is an injustice? I don't care. I'm the one that decides on who gets what! It's me that gives out the stuff! Because I have the power of Charity!"

"The power of Charity? You are telling this to me? To ME!? I, who am here, sitting on the High Backed chair! To me, dressed with diamonds, rings, gold—you are telling this to me, who owns castles and palaces? I have soldiers, I have prisons and I make laws. I send soldiers against those who scuff my shoes—I stomp on their heads!!! Non sum dignus?

"You dare tell me, Innocent III, that I do not have a right?! Oh, now you reveal your true face, Francis! You are worse than that smiling Pietro Valdo, the heretic, you are ... Ah, ah, I am sick ... please, forgive me, Francis, forgive me, but I fail to understand. What are you saying? Or, rather, of course I understand it, but I cannot accept it. I will never accept it. If you must spout these pearls of wisdom, then cast them before swine! Go to a pigsty and regale the pigs with your priceless wisdom! Yes, go away! Go to the pigs, Francis! Talk to them, they will listen to you and they will understand you. Go, Francis! Go! Go!"

"Oh, thank you, thank you, Holy Father, for this wisdom!"

Francis goes out into the courtyard and calls his companions: "Brothers, let's go! The Pope gave me the most wonderful advice. I would never have thought of it. He is not the Pope for nothing! Come, we must speak to the pigs. We must fly!"

The friars leave Rome and set off for the countryside. When they get to a field,

FRANCIS CALLS on the POPE

Francis says: "Ah, there, do you smell it? Unless my nostrils deceive me, there is a big beautiful pigsty right over there. Wait here, boys. I'll go alone."

As he enters the pigsty, he is faced with a fat, grunting sow with many boobs. Behind it looms a huge oinking male pig and all the other pigs in the family.

"My splendid pigs! Brothers!" says Francis, with outstretched arms, "I come here by order of the Pope, who has instructed me to talk to you about the Gospel, Charity and the love that we should have for each other!" The pigs look at Francis with their eyes wide open. Francis kisses the pigs, embraces them, and rolls in the dungy mud with them.

Then, all covered in pig poop, he runs and jumps and bounds toward the city with his shocked companions following behind at a distance. When they arrive at the Pope's Palace, the guards sniff the air ... and disappear. Francis enters the palace, dashes up the stairs and enters the grand hall. The Pope is seated at dinner with some very distinguished personages—noblewomen, princes and Cardinals— conversing, laughing and raising their glasses. When Francis appears, a woman sniffs: "God, it stinks in here! Where is that blast of stench coming from?"

"Holy Father, I owe this ecstasy of the pigs to you!"

Francis walks, smiling, towards Innocent.
"Marvelous Pope! Thank you for the great gift you have given me! I went where you ordered me to go: among the pigs. How wonderful! I have embraced them, I have rolled around in the dung with them—just as you ordained, Holy Father, and they have indeed listened to me. I am so happy! Holy Father, I owe this ecstasy of the pigs to you!"

Francis is out of his mind with joy; he is dancing and jumping; he cartwheels down the hall—and—splat! splat!—pig poop flying all over the place. The sniffing woman throws up in her soup. Innocent raises his arm to command the guards to seize Francis, but Cardinal Colonna, grabs his arm.

"What are you doing, Innocent? What do you aim to do? Arrest him; throw him into prison? Be careful, Innocent, Francis is not

FRANCIS CALLS on the POPE

alone: he has brothers and sisters; he is father and mother to thousands and thousands of people. They are captivated by him, they would go to any length for him... he instills a passion you could never muster in two thousand years!"

"Yes, but he..."

"It's your fault. He took you at your word. He thinks you're infallible. You provoked him and he went. What are you going to do, Innocent? Beat him up? Kill him? Well, do what you like; do it! You will see what will happen! The war against Pietro Valdo will look like a walk in the country! The sea will turn to blood, the mountains will teeter and fall and crush Rome—you will see! Don't let me stop you!"

"Okay, big shot. You're the Papal counselor. So, counsel."

"Forgive him! Forgive him and above all embrace him!"

"Embrace him? He's covered in pig ... dung!"

"That's because of you!"

Innocent takes a deep breath and walks towards Francis, embraces him and hugs him to his bosom:

"Francis, forgive me! Forgive me, for I did not understand the wonderful folly of your mind."

Then he addresses his august guests:
"Now listen to me, you princes, Cardinals
and Bishops. From this moment on, I grant
Francis, and his companions, the right to go
where he wants to preach what he wants. He
can speak the Gospels wherever he chooses,
however he chooses. Furthermore, he and
his followers are permitted to live on charity.
Go now with my blessing, Francis! I give you
permission for your Rule. You have my word.
You'll get it all in writing."

"Oh, Holy Father, thank you, thank you!
Brothers, we have permission! Our most
fervent prayer has been answered!"

Francis and his brothers run out and find
the nearest square. Francis loses no time
and jumps up on a market stall:

"Romans, hear me: I am Francis from
Assisi. Let me share the joy I have
in my heart. The Pope bad me to
go commune with the pigs, and
I went to the pigs. I spoke to the pigs
directly from my heart. I told them we are
all creatures of God, brothers in Christ,
and the pigs, they truly listened to me.
The pigs understood."

"Who is this clown?"

"He's mad. Look at the way he's
dressed."

"What's he talking about—Christ? God?
The pigs and the Pope?"
"My God, he stinks!"

❧

"Get thee to a bathhouse!"
"No, brothers, sellers and buyers! Stop your
selling and buying just for a moment! The
Pope himself ..."
"He's demented ... talking about the Pope
and pigs in the same breath!" "Blasphemer!"

"God raises you with His hands and gives you flight!"

"If I could but beg a minute of your
precious time ..."
A man picks up a stone and throws it at
Francis and hits him in the eye.
"Ow! All right! I understand, today is not
the day!"
He scrambles down from the stall and
swiftly quits the market square with his
brothers.

They pass through Rome's main gate and soon find themselves in the fields. It's almost sunset when Francis' companions drop, exhausted to the ground and fall fast asleep. Francis stands under a vast tree—its enormous branches full of leaves spreading like open arms. Little birds hopping and chirping, flying around looking for a good perch to spend the night. Francis looks up at them:

"Oh, birds, how blissful you are, what a marvel! So light you are, and overflowing with joy. You don't have a care and how you fly, flapping your wings in the wind, so easily and in harmony. This air which is so close to God; surely it is His very breath. Perhaps the breeze itself is God ... and the wind is the Lord. God raises you with His hands and gives you flight!"

While Francis speaks his impromptu prayer, flocks of birds arrive from all around, birds of all kinds: finches, crows and hawks, even buzzards and eagles from the mountains and birds from the sea and the rivers. The tree fills up with birds—so many that you can't see a single leaf—and they all listen:

"Oh, blissful birds, free and light, who thrive without possessions, without burdens to weigh you down and no authority to enslave you! Oh, if men could only be so

FRANCIS CALLS on the POPE

light, without gluttonies crushing us down to our basest levels. We brag, full of greed, and thirst for possessions, and hunger for glory; we become crazed to overpower each other, clambering on other people's heads more macho and tough than everybody else. Lies! Rogueries! Wickedness and poverty of love! If we could but throw off these heavy shackles of greed and free ourselves of this wretched gluttony, we would surely levitate into the sky, and the whispered secret of a child would be enough to give us flight!"

Francis turns slightly and notices that, on the wide road behind him, a crowd of people has gathered. Women sob quietly not to break the spell, and men hold their breath unable to applaud.

Francis looks up at the sky: "How strange this world is, oh, Lord! To make people listen, some days, you must speak to the birds!"

FRANCIS

and the

SULTAN

of

ZIME AL BENY

rancis, soon after he had imparted the good Rule to his brothers, heard from deep inside himself, a calling, a beckoning to Palestine, a place called the Holy Land not only by the Christians but by the Muslims too. What a coincidence that both Jesus and Mohammed should be born in the same place!

French and German Christians on Genoese ships had conquered much of the coastline driving out the Muslims. Now they were preparing to liberate Jesus' Holy City with more bloody sacrifice on both sides.

Francis and two friars made their way to the port of Ancona from where they would embark on their voyage. But they had not reckoned on being denied passage just because they were broke. Francis never had any cash but he did have a few tricks up his sleeve. Each brother grabbed a sack of grain from the pier and pretending to be porters swung the sacks over their shoulders and went aboard the bragozzo, a two masted ship, ready to set sail ship to Syria. Sneaking around like three crafty crows, they hid themselves in the bottom of the ships' hold.

One of the brothers prayed:
"Saint Michael, please, help
us! You, who protect the
thieves and illegal
immigrants!"
But it wasn't long
after they had cast off
that a sailor discovered them. "What
maggots have we here?" He kicked
them up on deck and dragged Francis
and the friars before the captain.
"Ah wretched stowaways! Throw
them into the sea!" the captain ordered.
The sailors grabbed the friars like rag bags,
ready to hurl them into the deep.
"Have mercy!" cried the friars.
"We don't know how to swim!"
"Don't worry, little brothers. You will learn
right away. No charge for the swimming
lesson. Into the sea with them! And then get
back to work!" barked the captain.

Suddenly, out of the blue, an eerie glow lit
up the sky. A whipping wind raged, raising
great waves rolling across the deck like
breakers left over from Noah's Flood.
"Lower the mainsail!" shouted the captain.
But before the words had left his mouth, all
the sails were torn away billowing in the sky
like sheets hung out to dry.

The wind sheared the ship of its rigging and sails. The tumult of waves swept the main deck. The sailors rushed below.

Francis and his two friars clung to the main mast for dear life while they were clobbered by thrashing waves and gusts of wind strong enough to strip the skin off a billy goat. The ropes they tied around each other dug into their flesh and made them look like human salami.

"We are doomed. God save us!"

The sea's convulsions went on for a whole day and night.

At dawn, from the poop deck, the face of a sailor appeared; fixing his eyes onto the horizon. In a terrified voice, he shouted:

"Sea stack straight ahead!"

Other voices joined his:

"Cliff at the bow!"

"There's no way out! We are going to crash!"

"We are doomed."

"God save us!"

"God forgive us!"

FRANCIS and the SULTAN of ZIME AL BENY

Francis broke free from the ropes that bound him to the mast. He removed his billowing friar's cloak and threw it into the air, stepped on its hem, and grabbed both sides and then held on for dear life. His cloak swelled into a great sail. The length of cloth, forced by the wind coming from the coastline, became swollen like a great sail. The barge was going around in circles but finally turned about and went offshore.

"Miracolo! Miracolo!" shouted the chorus of sailors who came out to behold this wonder.

And the whole crew came out to rejoice.

Everyone rushed to embrace Brother Francis, but the captain forbad it: "Do not touch him! Francis is our mainsail now. He is keeping us on course. Do not disturb him."

Thus, poor Francis was obliged to keep his arms thrust up and out like the statue of a saint, framing his cloak as a sail to propel the precarious vessel to safety.

When at last the wind had calmed down, the captain bellowed: "Little Brother Francis, turns out you're quite a sailor. You can lower your arms now. I don't know where we are but thanks to you, we are out of Leviathan's mouth."

But Francis couldn't move his arms back

down. His joints felt nailed, locked into place into the shape of the cross.

Just as the crew began to relax into its old routine, once again the wind blew contrary. The battered ship spun and catapulted on zig-zagging currents. When land was finally sighted, shouts of "Hallelujah!" went up even from the captain. But these shouts for joy were soon replaced by disbelief: the sailors and the friars on the barge found themselves back at the same port of Ancona!

Disembarked and sickened by the great tossing on the ship, Francis was vomiting ceaselessly; the sea wasn't his element.

A knight, at the pier saw the friar staggering like a drunken sailor, and sneered:

"You're a demon jinx! You steer the ship back where you started from."

Francis whose humility was only matched by his wit, was about to burst out laughing at the knight's mockery, but instead of a laugh, a belch issued forth which was immediately followed by a projectile of vomit over the knight's fancy uniform.

Without hesitation, Francis tried to clean him with his sackcloth.

"I seem to be just as much a jinx on land! Oh, I beg your pardon, Sir Knight. I meant no disrespect."

FRANCIS and the SULTAN of ZIME AL BENY

But before he could finish his apology, VAZOOOM!

Another jet of vomit ...

All the sailors and fishermen on the pier burst out laughing so hard they wept and hiccupped out of control.

One of the sailors said:

"Don't you listen to him, Little Friar. You go to Palestine. You are needed there. You saved us; maybe you will save them. Besides you are the best jester at sea." "Between your humor and your inner fountain, the Muslims will either withdraw out of hilarity or disgust."

As each sailor took leave, he gave Francis a brotherly slap on the back.

After Francis managed to get his land legs back, he ventured forth again towards Palestine. This time he made it but we do not know how he got there, or by which ship he made the crossing.

Two friars, Simon and Lauro, traveled with Francis to pay his call on the Sultan.

The reason for another such torturous mission across the seas was simple: Francis needed to see with his own two eyes how Christians and Muslims who have such a close blood line could be slaughtering each other.

"We are all children of Adam and Eve. Can it really be that Faith which sustains us

121

together can drive us to mutual annihilation? If I can only speak to our Muslim brothers the true word of Jesus Christ who wants us all to be brothers, surely there will be a chance for peace," he shared his cheer of peace with his brothers.

"Let us both Christians and Muslins erase from our minds every trace of evil and replace it with an open embrace of love towards one another."

"I am positive," Francis kept saying, "our Muslin brothers are neither bad nor unfaithful. But how can they know the wisdom of Jesus if nobody has ever taught them the Gospel?"

As Francis and his two friars arrived at Damietta (which the Arabs called Zime al Beny) the Crusaders lay ruthless siege to the city. Francis attempted to engage them in Christian conversation, but all these warriors of Christ ever talked about, was the money they had plundered, the women they had raped, and the men they had speared and quartered.

"I must speak to the Sultan immediately. It is our only hope! Come!" Francis blurted out.

"How are we supposed to manage that trick?" Simon asked.

"Between us, Francis, and the Sultan's palace are many guard posts and hundreds of soldiers," Lauro warned. "Do you really expect these Christian warriors lurking in the shadows to show us the way?"

"How did we make it to Palestine, my brothers?"

"Only by God's grace," answered Simon.

"That was the only way we made it," agreed Lauro.

"Okay, then. We will use the same method to the Sultan's palace."

"But Francis, tonight there will be a full moon spreading light like a hundred beacons shining on our every step!"

"With so much heavenly light, there is no reason to be afraid."

That night as the sun set, the moon was shrouded by a black shadow and encircled by a blood red halo.

123

"The world is ending! Run for the caves!"

The bravest soldiers, terrified, threw down their weapons and cried out:

"Eclipse! The sign of the bloody Apocalypse is upon us!"

"The world is ending! Run for the caves!"

And from the battlements Arab cries go up:

"A curse, a curse has been leveled against our people from on high. Run for the caves!"

Meanwhile Francis and his two little friars pass unmolested and unobserved through the twisting streets. One guard post after another lay abandoned and silent. They don't even come across a lost dog.

After turning this way and that, a grand palace appears before them with magnificent arches. "You see, my brothers. What did I tell you? It was a breeze. And you were worried!"

"Who are you, people? State your business!" demands a voice from the darkness.

"We are friars."

"Friars? What kind of thing is a friar?"

"Just simple friars!"

"Well then, what are you waiting for? Come

in, and do help yourselves, simple friars!"

A lamp of ten candles is lit and ... who should appear? The Sultan himself: Al-Malik al-Kamil.

"You are Francis," the Sultan says, not as a question but as a statement, pointing his finger towards the Holy One.

And Francis in return:

"You are Al-Malik al-Kamil ... I have heard some good stories about you."

"Me too, about you, Francis! May I offer you and your friends a jar of fresh water?"

Francis and his friars, parched from the heat, drain jug after jug. Francis pours a bucket of water down his gullet and then, taking a deep breath, exclaims:

"How good and gentle is this spring water. Gurgling down inside my body! It is so pure and without smell, they say, but I myself find that it has the most delicate of flavors."

"This is true," the Sultan agrees with him.

"Consider, my new friend, how much every man is driven to find pleasure; he works himself to the bone in search of ginger liquors, sweet and rare essences, and claw at each other's throat to obtain them ... They can't get it into their head that no delicacy is better than pure spring water!"

"You are so right" says the Sultan. "We also know these fussy eaters always looking for more and more refined and sophisticated food and drink. But in truth, they have neither eyes to discern nor palate to taste."

FRANCIS and the SULTAN of ZIME AL BENY

"But perhaps the worst, dear Sultan, are those wise and great scholars inside our monasteries, who from their high windows denounce the world and all creation with disgust. They say:

'Don't bother living in this universe since this life is false, it's only vanity and delusion. We creatures pass through this vale of tears merely as a waiting room to the real world, just on the other side of bodily death.'"

The Sultan is listening very carefully; whispering in his ear, a scribe is translating Francis' words into Arabic.

Many Muslims come to listen and surround the Sultan and the friars at a distance.. The Sultan nods for them to come closer.

Francis quenches his thirst with more delicious spring water, and then continues:

"Blessed is the man who discovers the small things of creation. The ones most to be cherished, while the foolish man scorns them since they don't cost a penny. Think how precious is the air we breathe, the air which moves and forms the wind, which causes the fronds of our trees to sway, the sails to fill and the waves of the sea to flow. You don't pay for the wind: yet you can't find a more precious thing. Or, consider Fire which warms us, makes iron red-hot to forge our tools and bakes clay for our vessels and pots!"

⚜

"Silence, Christian! Enough!" interrupts a Holy man of Allah. "You, with your idiotic rigmarole—you think this act impresses us? It is time instead for us to enlighten you! All your revelations can be found in the Qur'an, expressed in a more poetic way. You, pathetic Friar, you've come all this way to our land to convince us that your God is the only Lord, the Holiest and the only Creator? Maybe where you come from, people are taken in by your fraudulent sermons and your fancy footwork, but here they are quite useless. If you want to convince us that the Christian religion is the best, and that our God and all the prophets of Allah are liars and are to be rejected, let me tell you a secret. This is the biggest waste of breath! Unless, of course, you wish to submit to the divine Judgment of Fire?"

Francis opens his eyes and ears wide: "The Judgment of Fire? What does that mean?"

"It means this: two long stacks of wood set end to end are lit on fire. When they are glowing hot as Hades the two of us, you and I, one after the other, go for a little stroll across the burning flames. The one, who catches fire and gets roasted like a billy goat, he proves that his God is a total fraud! That false god must be erased at once from the Book of Life. It will be clear to everyone this God does not and never did exist. Only one God creator will remain in heaven: the one of the winner!"

Good Francis thinks over the Holy Man's proposition:

"This challenge of the fire truly excites me. Just think of the satisfaction I will enjoy in the crossing of this procession of hell, if I walk out the winner! Everyone in my home town of Assisi will bow down to me. Even the Pope himself will have to kneel in front of me. Your kind invitation in that respect is irresistible. And I wish to accept."

"You do?"

"Yes, but one thing nags at me."

"I thought so."

"Perhaps you can help me clear it up. Does it not smack of overweening pride that I, lowly Francis, could ever presume to be the savior to my Lord, the Creator? Instead of the other way around? Do I dare grasp the banner with the insignia of the cross!"

The Holy Man of Muhammad roars with laughter.

"My cunning fellow, you fill the air with double talk—not over high minded principles, mind you, but based on the lowest minded principle of all: Say it! You are afraid! You came here to teach us the truth, but it is we who will teach you the truth. Prepare yourself! The truth is this: You have no trust in your God. Your God cannot save you from the fire, because your Christian God does not exist! And I tell you, my dear little wily friar, your reputation as a blessed soul is just as much a joke!"

"Only one God Creator will remain in heaven: the one of the winner!"

Francis smiles but cannot disguise his indignation:
"Holy Man of the Mohammedans, you really wish to mortify me with insults? If it is fire you desire, you have lit the spark inside me. You leave me no choice! I am obliged to take to the field. Lord Sultan, if you grant us this clash of divine judgment, I am ready ... Let the trial begin!"

At once a group of men appear with heavy bundles of wood in the shape of a long track. On and on the track goes and finally they set it on fire.

"What happens if neither of us escapes the flames? The whole sky will be consumed by fire."

Francis kisses and strokes the cheeks of his two young friars who weep like fountains. He then gently embraces the Holy Man and tells him:

"While waiting for the blaze to heat up, there is one outcome, my friend, which perhaps you have not considered. What happens if neither of us escapes these flames? What happens then? You and I both end up roasted. The whole sky would be consumed by fire: of the two Gods, neither remains. Both our Creators would be erased from the Book of Life! To whom do Muslims and Christians pray? Now that you and I have emptied the sky? To whom do we

ask forgiveness for our sins? To whom do
Muslims and Christians apply for a miracle?
Have you thought about the staffing
problems? The redundancies! If there is no
God, what are we going to do with priests,
bishops and the Pope, not to mention your
imams and holy Fathers? What's the point of
interceding with gods who don't exist. Think
of the real estate glut that would ensue. The
cathedrals, churches and mosques remain
empty and bare ... Can you imagine! And
your muezzin, what will he be singing on the
high tower, as nobody is listening anymore
and no one will go down on their knees?
Paradise becomes null and void even before
our embers here grow cold! Angels, and
even devils, will become old age pensioners
in nursing homes. The guilt for every
turpitude and wickedness would be ours and
only ours. Consider it well, Holy Man!"

   At this point, the Holy Man of the Muslims,
a little dumbfounded, gawks at Francis
   "Oh, devilish cunning Friar that you are,
what a shame you will not survive the trial
because you would have had a brilliant
career as a comedian on stage. You have
missed your calling! You don't scare me with
this amusing paradox because both of us will

131

not roast, because my Lord Allah, you can swear on it, will save me, and only you will remain roasted in the flames."

✠

"I surrender: I will roast and your little tootsies, will be spared. Only the poor Christians will be deprived of their God. Imagine the outrage at having been duped for all these centuries. Thank God, I won't be around to hear the complaints at the central office."

"Well, as long as that's clear, little friar, we will have held up our end of the bargain," said the Holy Man.

"You are holding up the whole sky! No, there is nothing to be done but for us all to become Muslims."

"Excuse me?"

"Because Allah is here, there and everywhere! He is unavoidable."

"That is of course true—at least for the faithful."

"Oh, I can see them now: the multitudes of new ex-Christian believers crossing the sea on a thousand ships and prostrating themselves on these shores: "Allah, Allah! Give us Allah!" The lines outside every mosque will go on for miles.

"No wait is too long to worship Allah. But his way is strict."

"If I know my Christian brothers they
will get along just fine with the rules and
precepts of the Qu'ran."

"Many fall by the wayside!"

"Who doesn't want to take on a new wife?
And then another younger model? And then
an even younger one? Such a multitude
of males of former Christians in heat will
be flooding down here like a typhoon of
men ... But not to worry, Holy Man, I'm sure
there will be a few girls and little old ladies
left for you. Hallelujah, let the weddings
commence!"

"The Muslim wedding ritual is a very sacred
tightly regulated event."

133

"Who said it wasn't? However, this is nothing but a harbinger of the chaos about to appear on your doorstep!"

"Chaos? What chaos?"

"Well, take the whole pork issue. We all understand how strictly Allah has forbidden his followers to eat pork. But soon you'll discover the cleverness of these Christian converts. You think I am wily? Wait until you have met some of my brothers when he has a taste for ham! Soon these rascals will make masks of calves and sheep heads to put over the faces of piglets. They will even teach the young piglets to bleat and bellow so that you Muslims too will eat ham and pork rinds like native Venetians, convinced with every bite that you are eating sheep and lamb! No idea at all you are committing a mortal sin."

"This is a ridiculous theory, Christian! You might as well tell me that soon we will be drinking wine."

"I'm not saying how soon. And the prohibition against alcohol is so strict."

"No exceptions!"

"None. Except when my Christian brothers feed the lambs and goats red juicy grapes which will ferment in the animals' stomachs. Two weeks later when you go to milk sheep and goats, each squeeze of the udders will spurt out some very excellent wine. Then you will pour it down your throats. Soon you will be laughing your heads off, my dear Muslims, guzzling this pink and fragrant milk ... how you will dance and sing Allah's praises: "Allah! Allah! and Holy Muhammad, the perfect faithful is the drunken man!"

The Holy Man of the Arabs now bursts out sobbing, grits his teeth, gets on his knees and bangs his head on the floor until it rattles with loose parts.

The Sultan approaches his holy man, puts an arm around him and leans over:

"Perhaps it's better we forget about the trial for today. Let the fire consume the wood. You are not at all wrong, Holy Man. But for today, this simple friar has saved for making a mess of religion."
the Sultan orders his
"We have built a great fire.
and quarters of beef ...

FRANCIS and the SULTAN of ZIME AL BENY

roast them instead of men. Let the musicians play their instruments to spread harmony between Muslims and Christians. And you, beautiful females, won't you offer us your sultry dances. Let us join in the merrymaking for our mutual great fortune, which gives us two Father Creators for the price of one!"

When the multitude of Muslims had begun
to feast, Francis stood apart by a window,
and staring up at the moon, confides:
"My Lord, surely this very instant you
are sitting on that globe of light frowning
down at me ... Please, forgive your servant
for playing the fool about creation, and
making crude jokes against our doctrine
and religion. But it was all for a good cause,
don't you see? To avoid me being burned
to smithereens and your disappearing from
the sky! In my defense, if I overdid it, it's
your fault. Yes, yours, Heavenly Father.
Who created me bursting at the seams with
buffoonery? Take my storytelling and have a
loud laugh!"

FRANCIS and the SULTAN of ZIME AL BENY

VIII

FRANCIS

on the

ROAD

to

DEATH

Saint Francis is now forty-odd years old, but he looks like a decrepit old man. His flesh is prey to every disease you can think of—pains in the stomach, a bad liver, tears of blood in his eyes, trembling marsh fever—but Francis never stops; he never rests.

His brothers reproach him:

"Francis, won't you, for God's sake, stop!
With all the illnesses that plague you, you
need your rest! Relax or drop dead!"

But, Francis will not rest! If a hurricane
tramples down the wheat, he goes down to
the fields to help the peasants with what's
left of the harvest. If a fire blazes through
the forests, he runs to help the scorched and
desperate victims.

"No, I can't stop, I must go and earn the
alms our peasants give us. Get it into your
heads we are not freeloaders. We cannot be
fed and clothed by the peasants who barely
scrape a living out of the soil! Do not be
afraid to labor with your arms and back. We
can't expect these poor people to slog for

us just because we say our pretty prayers and chant glory to God. Do we do nothing but sing while the peasants do nothing but grind away?"

Day after day, Francis starts out for the fields, his eyes worn out. And finally his back won't hold him up. One day the inevitable befalls him, and his brothers find him unconscious in the field.

"Brother Fire, please be gentle: do not kill me too much."

The brothers decide to take Francis to a famous doctor. One brother says:
"There lives in Gubbio a renowned healer, a doctor at the university! ... "
So they set off for Gubbio, carrying Francis on their backs ...

The famous doctor takes one look at Francis and bursts out: "Oh, brothers, why did you wait so long? Look at the state this poor fellow is in! I must cauterize him forthwith!"

HOLY JESTER!

"Absolutely! Cauterize him. Sounds good," says one brother.

But another brother asks: "Cauterize? What exactly does that involve?"

"It means, Fire, dear friars," replies the famous doctor. "I will apply my famous red hot iron bars to his temples near the eyes so as to scorch the infected matter. There is no time lose!"

Immediately one of the brothers faints. Another flees in terror.

Meanwhile, the surgeon has already plunged the iron into the fire. Francis murmurs:

"Brother Fire ... be kind, don't make me cry out with pain, please be gentle: do not kill me too much!"

Without warning, in one smooth motion, the doctor sears the glowing red iron to the sides of his eyes—smoke seems to come out of his eyes and the smell of burning flesh is everywhere.

Francis clenches his teeth; he trembles, he stamps his feet, but he doesn't scream—he endures the pain. In the end he is so pale that he seems bloodless.

Then the brothers hoist him back on

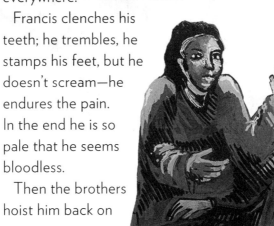

their shoulders and carry him away, not sure whether they are bearing his body or his corpse.

For three days Francis seemed somewhat revived, but before long he started bleeding again. Something must be done. The brothers confer:

"None of us will survive the famous red hot irons in Gubbio again."

"No, we must go to Siena to the best hospital with the best doctors in the world."

"It's a very long trip. Will the Master survive the trip?"

"Even so, he will not survive staying here. It's our last hope."

They prepare a stretcher made of two wooden dowels and a blanket. The four of them lift Francis onto the makeshift pallet for the long hike ahead. They walk along the Trasimeno Lake, till they arrive near Stranziano. It's here that Francis speaks his first words of the journey:

"Please stop. I know this place; nearby are the warm sweet springs of Bagno Rapo where we swam naked as boys. The springs may do me more good than the doctor. Please, my brothers, may we take this detour? There, you can see the vapor rising!"

"Yes, yes, Francis, we are
on our way right now!"

"But where is it? What's become of the
beautiful springs?"

"Look, Francis, it's been covered; hidden
under a rich cupola like a cathedral, with
palatial columns and arches.

"See how the steam escapes from the
top."

"Who has built a prison around the natural
springs?"

"Ah, the Earl of Gera stole it!" a passing
peasant explains. "The spring has always
belonged to the people, but the Earl said:
'It's mine.' He had this cupola built over it
to keep everybody out. Only he and his
friends are allowed to splash around naked:
everyone else: 'Keep out!'"

"But this is a devil's trick never seen
before!" cry the friars.

"You cannot hog for yourself what the

145

Lord has planted for everyone. The people must stick up for their rights!"

"A delegation must be dispatched to the Bishop! We must revolt!"

"Calm down, brothers," counsels Francis, in a feeble voice. "Do you want to start a war over a splutter of warm water? Get a hold of yourselves! We will find another spring along the road. Pick up your clothes and let's go!"

Half-heartedly, the friars take to the road again with Francis on their shoulders.

Step by step finally they arrive in Siena without coming across another spring.

Just outside the town walls, they run into a multitude of friars coming from every direction who surround Francis. When they had learned Francis was on his way, they all came to embrace him.

"Brothers, be gentle," Francis says, "because, with this love of yours, you risk tearing me to pieces!"

The wise, skillful doctors of Siena have also come to greet him and escort him to the hospital. Immediately they set to covering him with plasters; they put red-hot cups on his chest to extract the toxic dampness from his body; for safe measure they stick blood sucking leeches on his back—little bloodsuckers! Every day they

HOLY JESTER!

repeat the ritual: plasters, cups, leeches. But Francis shows no sign of improvement.

One evening, at sunset, Francis is called by his visiting brothers to a big meadow. They have assembled in Siena to discuss Exceptions to the Rule; to amend it because, it turns out, the new pope and his Ministers don't like it. The first amendment on the agenda is to abolish the obligation to work. A friar would no longer need to earn his living and be worthy of alms.

The friars all begin expounding their own ideas in sweet, gentle voices but, as the discussion heats up, they are soon all shouting at each other at the top of their lungs using language they must have learned in the confessional.

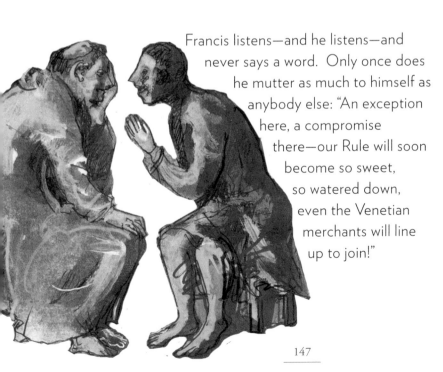

Francis listens—and he listens—and never says a word. Only once does he mutter as much to himself as anybody else: "An exception here, a compromise there—our Rule will soon become so sweet, so watered down, even the Venetian merchants will line up to join!"

FRANCIS on the ROAD to DEATH

Every day the doctors apply a new poultice but none of the treatments bring Francis any relief. It's all just pointless torture. He calls his brothers to his side:

"Please, brothers, take me home. I feel the life draining from my heart."

The brothers lift his frail body back on the stretcher and set off back from whence they had come. Again they pass near the Earl's private spring but, when they approach, the cupola and the columns have vanished! Broken columns are scattered along the shore. Exposed to the sky and the air again is the spring! Open-air! All free again!

The brothers cry: "What in heavens!"

"Soon after you left," says another passing peasant, "a tempest broke out that shook the cupola; then an earthquake made the columns tremble, then—ZAM!—a bolt of lightning struck the cupola and everything was flung up in the air like a volcano spitting lava."

"Hurrah, hurrah!" the friars shout for joy, jumping and dancing.

"It was God—God! who visited this punishment on those selfish cunning thieves! "Thank you, oh Lord! ... "

Francis claps his hands trying to get attention. His voice is so weak now that no one can hear him, so he waits for silence.

"Enough! Do you really think with all the troubles that weigh on the Eternal Father throughout the universe—stars blowing up,

"Who has built a prison around the natural springs!"

comets leaving their path, planets jumping out of the firmament—do you think he has spare time to punish those who put up columns around a little spring? Or those who trample on the rules and rights of others, thieves of any kinds? Can you imagine:

"You despotic nobleman, you have committed such foul deeds, I will teach you a lesson—take this earthquake! Let me hurl this tempest at you! You, Lord of Thieves—take this lightning bolt! Think about it: there would never again be a single day with a clear sky! We must just thank Him for what has happened and simply float happy as children in the water!"

The brothers all strip naked, enter the spring, sing, laugh, splash around like children; gently, they bathe Francis in the water ... and he too laughs a little. Refreshed, they set off again for Assisi.

They soon pass through a village where all the villagers run joyfully towards Francis:

"Francis! Francis, stay here with us! We'll give you a big house for you and your brothers!"

"I am sorry," says Francis, "I thank you with all my heart, but we must go straight back to Assisi."

When they pass through another little town it's the same story: all the people gather around Francis:

"Oh, sweet Francis, our guardian, remain here, gladden our hearts, we'll give you the grand old castle—all for you!"

"How very nice, but we can't, they are waiting for us at home. We are already running late!'

Among the brothers there is a young novitiate who exclaims:

"Ah, the rewards of a blessed life! How wonderful everybody welcomes Francis to stay with them!"

"My son, they don't want Francis to stay here; they want him to die here."

"Surely, not!"

"They have already drawn up the plans for a lofty cathedral to mark the spot. It's good for business my boy. Move on! Move on!"

Step by step, the friars make their way to the plain below Assisi where Francis asks his brothers to accompany him to Porziuncola—the little church so loved by Francis. They begin to change route when mounted soldiers intercept them:

FRANCIS on the ROAD to DEATH

"Not that way! We'll take it from here. We are in charge now. We will protect Francis!"

"Protect him from what? From whom? Everyone loves him!"

"Bandits are everywhere who want to take Francis hostage: they will deliver him to the town that pays the biggest ransom to earn the sacred place of glory and honor."

And Francis says in a whisper: "They want me to die everywhere?! I've got half a mind to not die at all!"

The brothers follow the soldiers up the hill and enter Assisi.

The Bishop of Assisi, Guido, who had known Francis since he was a child, embraces him:

"At last, Francis, you have come home. Welcome! Come into my palace."

He puts Francis in a big bed in his own corner room. It is the most plush and comfortable bed he has ever felt beneath him, but as much as he longed to fall into the

arms of slumber, he cannot. The mattress is too soft—he sinks into the bed, and tosses and turns:

"Brothers, take me off here ... I am drowning in feathers ... "

They lift him off the bed and lay him on the cold hard floor and, with a deep tranquil sigh, he exclaims:

"Oh, yes! Now I am in my place. This is the life!"

Down below, around the palace, the soldiers take turns on watch. All around the perimeter, squads of armed men stand at alert to protect the Saint from being kidnapped. Francis, lying there on the floor, calls to his brothers:

"Please, brothers of mine, do me a favor ... a great sadness envelops me ... the river of strength that has flowed through my heart is running out ... please, grant me one final gift."

"Anything that can be done, we shall do for you, Francis. Name it."

"Intone for me a sweet, cheerful song."

"A song! That's it? Yes, surely, Francis. Which one?"

"The one that goes, 'Glory to the Lord ... for brother Sun."

"Oh yes, The Canticle of the Brother Sun. Let's do it! Let's pitch our voices, please."

They position themselves around Francis:

"You, first voice ... "

"AEOHH!"

FRANCIS on the ROAD to DEATH

"Good. You go over there. Second voice, please ... "

"AEOOOUU-AHA!"

"Good, you stay here. Third one! Hold the note, let me hear you ..."

"AEOUH!"

"That's fine, you stay there. Fourth one! ..."

"AEOOOUHA-GAINGA!"

"No, no, step back! Okay, stop there! Right: AAEEOO UU-AA! Now, let's start!"

All praise be yours, my Lord,
All glory and honor.
All blessing be yours, my Lord,
First through Sir Brother Sun
Who gives us the day and the light.
How beautiful he is, how radiant
In all his splendor!
Of You, the Highest,
He bears the likeness
And the glory ...

The soldiers on guard below the palace hear the singing:

"Hey! The Saint is croaking, but he's in darned good spirits!"

A priest says: "It doesn't seem proper ... breaking into merry song when you ought to be preparing yourself for a good death! Highly unbecoming for a saint!"

The singing continued through the night but, truth be told, by midnight Francis was no longer there. In fact, only four friars had remained to sing. As soon as the

sun had gone down, the other friars, on
Francis' order, had quietly transported him
through the servant's entrance out of the
palace. They crossed the city of Assisi via
underground tunnels, walked paths Francis
had known as a boy until they finally arrived
at the Porziuncola.

It is here that Francis had asked to die.
The brothers lay him on the earthen floor.
He looked up towards the roof ripped wide
open:

"What a sky! Sprinkled with stars. What a
grand setting you have prepared for me! Oh,
thank you, my Lord, thank you!"

And he begins to sing, in a voice that
grows softer, and softer, until it becomes a
mere whisper:

"All praise be yours, My Lord,
For our sister Bodily Death
That no one can escape.
The second death will do us no harm
If we are prepared in spiritual peace.
All praise be yours, My Lord,
For this sweetness
That you give to us
In our last breath.
All praise be
yours, My Lord!"

—Finis—

> "Pirovano is a self-taught actor of great expressive quality. I found him exceptional. He showed a vitality that was all his own, and the energetic inventiveness of a great storyteller"
>
> – Dario Fo.

In 1983, Mario Pirovano was living and working in London when he met Dario Fo at a performance of Fo's masterpiece, *Mistero Buffo*. The two men sparked an instant friendship, and despite having no previous theatrical background Pirovano has acted and/or participated in every single work produced by Fo and Franca Rame. Pirovano's uniquely close and long-standing personal and professional relationship with Fo makes him one of the playwright's most qualified interpreters.

MARIO PIROVANO

Over the last twenty-five years Pirovano has performed Fo's work in Italian and Spanish from Europe to North and South America, from China to Africa and Australia. Pirovano has also translated Fo's *Johan Padan and the Discovery of America*. In 2013, he translated Fo's versions of Ruzzante's monologues which Fo had re-conceived and performed in 1993.

This translation is dedicated to my wife Angela

DARIO FO

Dario Fo was born in 1926 in San Giano (Varese), North of Italy, near the shore of Lago Maggiore, where he learned storytelling from his grandfather and fishers and glassblowers. He studied art and architecture at university in Milan, but grew increasingly attracted to the theatre and left his studies to pursue stage design.

His father had helped Italian Jews and British prisoners of war escape into Switzerland. His mother devoted herself to wounded partisans who fought against Mussolini and the Nazi occupation forces.

HOLY JESTER!

Since the early 1950's, together with his wife, the actress Franca Rame, Fo wrote, produced and performed over eighty politically charged, satirical plays for the stage as well as radio and television, typically drawing on medieval or Biblical material; and the tradition of the Commedia dell'arte.

The couple set up a series of radical theatre companies, to connect with audiences outside the traditionally middle class theatre-going venues.

Though enormously popular with the masses, Fo's plays have regularly been censored by the Italian government and have earned Fo and Rame opposition from various political groups, chiefly those of the far right. Fo became persona non grata throughout communist Europe after rescinding the rights to all his plays in Czechoslovakia as a protest against the Soviet-led invasion.

In addition to *Holy Jester!*, he also wrote two other illustrated novels: *The Pope's Daughter* (Random House, 2014) and *There is a Mad King in Denmark*, 2015.

In 1997, Fo was awarded the Nobel Prize for Literature, at which time the Award Committee called him "the most performed living playwright in the world." "We've had to endure abuse, assault by the police, insults from the right-thinking and violence," Fo said in his Nobel lecture.

Fo's plays are published in over 50 countries and in more than 30 languages. His paintings and drawings have been exhibited internationally.

Highlights of Fo's career include: *Mistero Buffo* (1969); *Accidental Death of an Anarchist* (1970); *Johan Padan and the Discovery of Americas* (1992).

Dario Fo died on October 13, 2016 in Milan.